BLACK STAR, BLACK SUN

Black Star, Black Sun

Rich Hawkins

BLACK
SHUCK
BOOKS

Black Shuck Books
www.blackshuckbooks.co.uk

First published in Great Britain in 2015 by April Moon Books

978-1-913038-24-3

To my father.
I miss you, Dad,
but I hope to see you again in some place.

*"I have seen the dark universe yawning
Where the black planets roll without aim,
Where they roll in their horror unheeded, without
knowledge or lustre or name."*

Excerpt from 'Nemesis' by HP Lovecraft

Prologue

The people were out in the fields staring at the fluid sky, and some of them were on their hands and knees, squirming like larvae in the dirt. A few crouched, swaying on sore heels, eyes shut, mouths moving without sound. Others were dead, sprawled and twisted into cruciform shapes. The remaining villagers wept or screamed or laughed at a joke none of them understood.

Ben was curled foetal among them, damp earth in his mouth, tears on his face, and chemical filth in his veins. An old woman muttered nonsense words and raised her arms to the clouds. A man wiped his mouth until his lips were raw, and he grinned around bleeding gums.

Ben wrapped his arms around his chest as a growing numbness filled his limbs. A flock of birds swarmed in black droves over the field.

A groan within the earth. The sound of falling mountains. Distant thunder.

Salvation. Communion.

The black star.

One

Ben fed the steering wheel through his hands as the car rounded a corner in the narrow road. The windscreen wipers scraped upon glass and the rain fell in pattering waves, constant and thick, a soupy drizzle turning the light watery and meek. The car creaked and rattled as it swayed in the gusts dancing across the bare fields, back roads and winding lanes. He flicked on the headlights and frowned at the choking cough of the engine as it struggled up a steep incline. The stereo played Johnny Cash.

His legs ached. There was a dull throb under his forehead, a slight pressure behind his eyes, like pressing thumbs. He'd been on the road without a break since dawn. It had been a long drive south.

The car bumped over uneven tarmac and small potholes, flanked by spiked hedgerows and briar patches. Rainwater and wet gravel kicked up by the grind of tyres fighting for traction. Twisted trees with heavy branches grasped at the black sky. Oaks, yews and skeletal elms. Willows weeping to the ground. Trees fit for the hanging of men.

Ben's stomach fluttered and his muscles tensed. His chest felt like it was stuffed with chalk and dust squeezing his heart. His throat constricted, and he breathed through his nose to calm himself. Dry mouth. He licked his lips, checked the rear-view mirror, the road behind him as obscured as the road ahead of him, and exhaled until his lungs flattened into papery sacks.

The ground rose. Among the shallow hills the village was an ashen stain on the land, crowned by rain and low clouds. Greys and browns and shades of autumn slowly becoming winter. The light was already fading, as if the normal cycle of day and night had been discarded.

Ben swigged from the water bottle he kept nearby. Nicotine cravings needled under his skin. He passed a tall oak with gnarled and calloused limbs. Grass banks and ditches foamed with nettles and long grass the height of stunted children.

A road sign. *Marchwood*. Just the sight of the name made his heartbeat spike and adrenaline leak into his empty stomach. It made a bitter taste at the back of his throat.

He took the main road, past familiar houses and old side roads. The arteries and veins of the village. The road was a ribbon of grey, cracked tarmac and pot holes.

Past the village hall, the grocery shop, the butcher's, the Duke of York pub; St. Michael's church and the small school opposite it he had attended until he was eleven. The Miller family's farm. White cottages with thatched roofs. Telephone poles and the occasional phone box painted the red of childhood summers. An old water pump dwelled inside an alcove in a wall with *DO NOT USE* inscribed above it. Lines of cars parked by the sides of the road. The street narrowed and he had to pull over twice to give way to cars heading towards him. In the last few decades newer houses had been built to tempt retired couples from the cities.

Buildings sagged, crooked and leaning, and there were squat houses with bowed eaves and arched roofs; bungalows with red brick walls and neat gardens. Council houses and cul-de-sacs. Satellite dishes aimed for the heaving sky.

The dull streets were empty save for a tall man in a red waterproof coat walking a German Shepherd, and a limping woman with her head bowed against the downpour, laden with bulging plastic bags that pulled her arms towards the pavement so her gait was ape-like and unsettling. The man with the dog turned his head and stared at Ben's car until it passed down the road.

The rain fell harder, blurring the world through the windows. The sky opened up like a dark wound. Ben turned up the dehumidifier to clear the misted glass around him. Johnny Cash sung about walking the line. Gutters and drains swelled. Froth and foam. He squinted to discern the road ahead and slowed the car until it was almost at crawling speed.

Ben craved a cigarette. He breathed out through his teeth and scratched a patch of skin behind his ear. The longing for nicotine deepened, became an itch in the damp fallows of his brain. His mouth tasted of iron.

He was almost home.

~

Ben turned off the engine and sunk into the seat. Sweat beaded on his brow and the bridge of his nose. He turned to his right and looked up at the house from the roadside, partly-obscured through the window. The house was dark, curtains drawn, with the suggestion of weak light through hairline cracks.

There was a break in the rain and he unloaded his bags from the boot and then locked the car with one press of the fob. He pocketed the keys. Weighed down with his belongings, he stared at the house, hesitant, swallowing a bad taste in his throat. The street was quiet, although he sensed scrutiny from various windows; the twitch of a curtain, the glimpse of a white face. It was to be expected. A small village was fertile ground for gossip. He reckoned the whole of Marchwood knew what had happened.

He didn't care. He had nothing to hide. And even if he was still under suspicion he was past worrying about it. Eighteen months was a long time. He listened to the sound of water falling into gutters. A slow dripping and the not unpleasant smell of the road scrubbed by rain.

He opened the black metal gate. His old home was a weathered structure of roughcast walls, and dark windows set into the house like gouged holes. A small lawn cleaved by a stone pathway. The grass was patchy like the fur of a mangy animal. Flowerbeds without flowers and a row of thin shrubs wilting in the cold. A ramshackle bird table held together by rusted nails and encrusted with sunflower seeds and pale droppings.

There was an old swallow's nest from a previous summer tucked into the crook of an upstairs window. Cracked guttering hung from the outer wall, just one strong draught away from being ripped from its brackets.

Ben walked up the pathway. No movement in the windows. The front door was a dark stain with a brass handle.

Ben ran his hand over a section of the door that was scratched and weathered, and then knocked three times. He could smell damp and grass clippings. He waited, the straps of his bags chafing his arms and shoulders.

No answer.

He knocked again. Knuckles on wood.

A click in the door. The sound of a key being turned in the lock. Ben steadied himself, remembered to breathe.

The door opened. A haggard face of faded watercolour. Grey hair and a stubbly beard. Old dull eyes, rimmed by tortoiseshell-framed glasses and crowned by thick eyebrows, appraised him and widened in recognition. One corner of a dry mouth twitched like a bloodless cut trying to heal.

"Hey, Dad," Ben said.

His father sagged in the doorway, thin-boned and creased with age. Pot belly. Tattered cardigan and trousers. The years were scrubbing him from the skin of time. Steptoe-chic fingerless gloves.

"Hello, lad. You're early."

"I wanted to get here before nightfall."

"Very wise. How are you?"

"Fine."

His father glanced at the sky. "You better come in. It's going to rain again."

~

A pile of empty beer cans wilted in the overflowing bin. A tap dripped into the kitchen sink piled with dirty plates and bowls. His father swept crumbs from a wooden cutting board on the fading worktop and put a jam jar back in the fridge. The linoleum floor was stained and grimy around the edges. A ticking clock counted slow seconds. The kitchen smelled of old vegetables and Ben imagined the cupboards filled with sprouting potatoes, black toadstools and blooms of fungi. There was a water stain on the ceiling and a hairline fracture in one of the pale walls. The top of the microwave was furred with dust. The cooker had seen its best years.

His father filled the kettle at the sink.

Ben put down his bags. "The house hasn't changed much."

"Never does," said Dad.

Rain scratched against the windows. "I heard it's going to rain for the rest of the day."

"It's England," Dad said as he dropped tea bags into mugs and added milk. "All we get is bad weather. Jesus wept." He piled chocolate digestives atop a small plate. Ben watched his father limp around the kitchen. The kettle boiled. Steam writhed like little ghosts. Dad poured the tea and spooned three sugars into his steaming mug.

"Thanks for letting me stay," Ben said.

Dad looked at him over his glasses. A frown made of shallow furrows, like lines cut in pastry. "Don't be so stupid. It's nothing. Now go and put your bags away. When you come back down we'll have these cups of tea."

Ben shuffled his feet, finding it hard to look his father in the face. He craved a cigarette to clear his mind and calm his blood. The longing for nicotine became a pulsing black knot in his gut.

"Make yourself comfortable, Ben. Get your bearings."

"Okay. Cheers, Dad."

"Welcome home, my boy."

~

Ben struggled up the narrow stairway with his bags hooked over his shoulders and scraping the walls. Damp grey light came from a small window set halfway up the stairs. Shadows formed on his heels and followed him. The wallpaper was rough and old, and the carpet that covered the stairs was threadbare and old. He was sweating by the time he reached the landing his father's bedroom to his right, the spare room to his left and his old room straight ahead. He looked up at the closed attic hatch and remembered, as a boy, being terrified of it opening to reveal some grinning horror beckoning him up to the dark where he'd be smothered among the forgotten toys, old cutlery and dusty Christmas decorations.

Flaking paint on his bedroom door, the result of taping posters of his favourite footballers upon it when he was younger. He placed his hand on the doorknob and it rattled between his fingers like small bones in a jar. He stepped into stale air and the scent of furniture polish and linseed oil. He switched on the light. A pang of nostalgia hit him as he surveyed his old bedroom. Ancient wallpaper, faded to a colour a shade darker than white and peeling at the edges. There were small bare patches where he had picked away the paper as a boy. The fossilized nubs of Blu-Tack he'd used to stick posters to the walls. The skirting boards were a sickly shade of jaundice-yellow above a brown carpet, which was worn in some places and matted by forgotten stains. This had been his room for over two decades, where he had spent most of his teenage years wasting his time.

Splintered memories of watching horror films on the small television his parents bought him for his thirteenth birthday. He remembered lonely midnight masturbation and stashing porn magazines under the bed. Puberty had hit him hard. Brooding over girls and drowning in teenage angst while listening to Slipknot, Manic Street Preachers and Metallica. Nights of heartbreak in the glow of Lava lamps. An irrational misdirected rage at the world. An angry young man, like so many others dwelling in shuttered bedrooms and musky dens.

He wondered how much of his DNA was contained within the room; his skin cells, hair and blood. He imagined something born from the leavings of his body, malformed and mewling, dry and wispy, grasping blindly for him as he slept.

Ben closed the door and put down his bags. All that remained in the room was the bed, a cupboard, a chest of drawers, a bedside table with a lamp, and a small television placed on a wooden chair. He used to hang Airfix model planes on fishing lines from the ceiling. Spitfires, Hurricanes, Lancaster bombers and Messerschmitt Bf 109s. Tin soldiers and scavenged fossils had once lined the empty shelves.

The window, flanked by dark frayed curtains, looked out on the front garden and the wet street. He didn't recognise the cars in the driveways of the houses across the road.

He opened the window and lit a cigarette. Coils of smoke drifted outside to be taken by the wind.

Two

The living room was full of mottled shades even with the curtains wide open. Grey ambient light cringed from the glow of two standing lamps.

Ben sat on the sofa and dismantled a biscuit in his hands. Dad slumped in his patched and worn armchair on the other side of the room, side-on to Ben and facing the television. Low volume, like whispers behind the walls. An old western. Clean-cut cowboys and villains in black.

Dad blew on his tea. Ben tried not to look too long at the framed photos arranged on the mantelpiece and the walls. Photos of Ben through his youth. Baby, toddler, sulking teenager. A photo of himself and Emily on their wedding day made his scalp tingle and his heart climb into his throat. Other photos of his dead grandparents. Mum and Dad on holiday in Athens, tanned, giddy and smiling. Black and white images of Edwardian ancestors; his family was of working class Somerset stock, mostly farm hands, manual workers and labourers.

One photo of his mother caused a tremor on his lips, the final one taken of her, smiling wanly with Dad, Ben and Emily beside her gaunt form. Two weeks before she died in a hospital bed.

Ben looked away from the collected memories and down at his feet, then at his father.

"How are things, Dad?"

His father slurped tea and stifled a burp in one cupped hand. "Fair. The days pass quickly. You'll realise that when you get older. How was the drive down here?"

"Took longer than it should. There was an accident on the motorway."

"The usual, then."

"Pretty much."

"How much time off has your work given you?"

"As long as I need, they said. They've been pretty good about it all. There's enough money saved up to pay the bills for a while, so I don't have to rush back."

"I always taught you to put some money aside. Glad you listened."

"I was thinking of moving back here for good, Dad. Nothing left for me in Shrewsbury. Emily's family still treat me like I had something to do with what happened. Her parents hardly speak to me."

"It wasn't your fault," said Dad.

"I know."

Dad took a biscuit from the small table by his armchair. "Imagine what it's like for them."

"What about me? How do they think I feel?"

"I know, lad. His father looked out the window.

Rain slapped the glass. "Do the police still suspect you?"

Ben sighed, rubbed the skin under one eye. "I expect there're a few investigating officers who'd love to see me banged up. It's always the husband who's got something to do with it, isn't it? Right from the start they treated me like I was guilty."

"Time to let it go, lad."

"Easier said than done."

"You may never discover what happened to her. You can't let it poison the rest of your life."

"Bit late for that, Dad."

"Don't be melodramatic."

"I had a nervous breakdown in a supermarket; I collapsed and started crying in the frozen meat aisle. I'm medicated up to my eyeballs. I've been seeing a psychologist, for fuck's sake."

His father looked at him, face creased with disappointment, as though his tea had turned sour. Then he turned away.

Ben's pulse thrashed inside his skull. Knuckles of dull pain pressed behind his eyes. His temper had caused him trouble in the last few months. Flares of anger and bouts of self-hate. And then there was the temptation to take sharp little things and use them upon his skin again. He craved that release, the focus of pain somewhere else than inside his head. Anything to get him through the day.

He downed the rest of his tea and rose from the sofa. "Thanks for the drink. I'm going upstairs to read for a bit."

"Okay, lad."

He turned towards the door to the stairs.

"Ben," his father said.

"Yeah?" He didn't look back.

"Good to have you home, son."

~

The first night back in his old bed, shivering beneath the thin sheets that swaddled him upon the hard, lumpy mattress. The immersion heater in the airing cupboard on the far side of the room offered meagre warmth to a room without central heating. Sleep was elusive except for fitful lulls in which fragments of half-dreams spun in his mind. Snatched voices, forgotten names, and tightened grimaces across the small skulls of strangers. Ben stared at the ceiling, listening to spiders skitter inside the walls. Dad was snoring in the next room. Outside, the street was silent, turned to silver by moonlight. The rain had stopped and the sky had cleared.

How he wished Emily was lying beside him, sharing heat and comfort in the dark. He'd never felt so lonely, so lost, and his body seemed old and emptied out. He pawed at eyes moist and warm. His jaws loosened and he ground his teeth. The shadows were always darker when faced alone.

From elsewhere in the village, in other places of silence and dark, night creatures called and harked. The owls, the foxes, and the badgers in nocturnal flight, picking through gardens and streets and shying away from lighted windows.

Ben closed his eyes, pulled the sheets up to his chin and swallowed the knot in his throat.

~

He woke with the first wan light of the morning, his body stiff, aching and cold. Only a few hours' broken sleep overnight, disturbed by noises and imagined movements from a dream barely dreamed and not forgotten. He'd had a nightmare about being chased by pale figures that loped and capered in the brown-yellow glow of dusk across a ploughed field. He was glad he couldn't recall what had happened after the figures caught him and took his body to the ground.

He rose and dressed. Washed his Sertraline tablet down with a few mouthfuls of water from the glass on the bedside table. Then he checked his mobile; no missed calls or messages. A faint hope, however unlikely, that the police had contacted him with news they'd tracked down Emily or found her remains somewhere, washed up on a beach or discovered in a waterlogged ditch. At least he'd know, then. But hope was born and nurtured from not knowing. He hated hope even while he grasped onto it with all his strength. And why did he keep hoping? To keep the last sliver of hope next to his heart. A velvet box filled with ashes and topped with a rose. It was all he had.

The house was quiet as he padded downstairs. Dad was in the living room reading a newspaper. BBC News 24 was on the television. Some distant country was embroiled in civil war and a politician had been caught ushering prostitutes into his hotel room.

"Cornflakes or toast, if you want breakfast," Dad said, not looking up from the newspaper.

"Cheers. Think I'll just have a coffee and a cigarette."

"Have to eat something, lad."

"I'll be fine."

He made the coffee with three sugars. He went out to the back garden and stood by the fishpond, sipping the coffee and pulling on the cigarette under a sky of science fiction blue. The water was covered with netting to stop herons from preying upon the goldfish, and circled with small rocks, ornamental frogs, fairies and hedgehogs. Various pebbles picked up from beaches as mementoes. Gnomes grinned at Ben with their fishing rods and bright red boots. Conical hats of garish colours. Mum had loved her ornaments and garden decorations.

The back garden looked out onto a small field of scrubland and brush, separated by a wooden fence Ben's father had erected almost twenty years ago. Beyond the field were rows of houses. He could see distant figures in the gardens and glimpses of movement at some windows.

The fence had survived many storms, but its stubbornness had left it as a sagging thing of faded brown streaked with slimy lichen and moss tucked into the damp spots between wooden slats. The posts were loose in their holes. It needed a new coat of creosote and much repair from careful hands.

There was a dead blackbird on the lawn. Its head was gone and feathers had been ripped from its body to scatter on the grass. Mangled wings. One leg was missing. A little creature mauled by one of the neighbourhood cats and then discarded when its small, broken form had lost its appeal. Ben stepped away and emptied the rest of the coffee onto the ground. Before he went back inside he put the cigarette out on the wall and left what remained of it in the ashtray by the door.

~

The cold air turned his breath to mist. The sun was full and high, but weak. He pulled the woollen hat down over his ears then put his hands over his mouth and blew into them. He rubbed his palms together to generate some warmth in his skin.

There was more activity on the streets than yesterday. A few people walked the pavements with dogs or prams. Others walked alone. Ben passed the butcher's shop and the raw meat stink from within. The butcher, his striped apron stained with offal and the cleaver in his meaty hand wet with animal blood, nodded at Ben from behind the counter. Ben nodded back and kept walking, trying not to look at the gutted pig carcass hanging in the window.

He raised his head to take in the church's dark spire against the sky. The churchyard was just off the main road. Cars trundled past. A woman in a red Range Rover waved at him and he returned the gesture even though he had no idea who she was. He walked through the gates and onto the uneven stone pathway. He paused at the war memorial and went through the names inscribed into the stone. The silent dead. A wreath of plastic poppies still wet from yesterday's rain. He looked at the tall granite cross, which was set upon a plinth of three hexagonal steps, each one smaller than the one below. The shaft of the cross, square at its base, tapered upwards. If he were a religious man he might have put his hands together and whispered a prayer, but it was irrational to talk to something in which he didn't believe. His mother had always disapproved of what she called his 'rebellious atheism'.

His maternal grandfather was among the names listed. Harold Hobbs died during the invasion of Normandy. 1944. D-Day. One of the first paratroopers dropped behind enemy lines before the coastal attack by Allied forces. He was killed by a German sniper near some French village, the name of which Ben couldn't remember.

He walked the wiry path that dissected the churchyard. The grass between the gravestones was freshly cut and sodden. Grass clippings, leaf-mulch and pine needles. The trees were tall and spindly, bare crooked branches ending at pencil-thin fingers. In his youth, for dares set by his friends, he used to run through the churchyard at night. The other children used to say that pale figures capered among the headstones and lurked by the path waiting to snatch anyone foolish enough to enter. He remembered the terrifying thrill of bolting down the same path he was standing on now, in the dark, guided by the splintered lights of houses glimpsed through the trees on the other side of the churchyard.

Once, he'd told his friends he'd seen a tall man with a white face emerge from a dark recess at the back of the churchyard and chase him. They believed him, and his 'bravery' got him his first hand-job from Amy Shrimpton that same night around the back of the cricket pavilion.

He could hear crows but couldn't see them. The church tower loomed above him, spotted with lichen and scarred from rain and wind. Stained glass windows had lost their lustre. Stone gargoyles leered, blind eyes and contorted mouths. Grinning masonry grotesques.

In the pale shadow of the church, he left the path and moved slowly among the headstones, old graves and markers. Christian signs and dying flowers in clay pots. A wreath was a flash of colour on the dark grass. He stepped past a recent grave with fresh flowers and heartfelt notes. He recognised many of the names on the headstones, some of whom he'd known. He passed a freshly-dug grave ready for filling.

He stood over the graves of his paternal grandparents. Conrad and Matilda Ottway, buried alongside each other. Ben had barely known Conrad, just snatched memories of a middle-aged man with a thick beard and spectacles. Conrad died of heart disease when Ben was six. Sylvia passed away two years after Ben and Emily were married. He silently promised to buy some flowers for their graves.

His mother's grave was a little further down the gentle slope, towards the edge of the churchyard. He crouched by her resting place and placed one hand on the headstone. Dad cared for the grave and kept the grass around it trim and neat, and had also arranged a small pot of white lilies in water.

Ben placed his hand on the damp ground that was her grave. He missed his mother whenever he thought of her. She had just started her retirement when she was diagnosed, and the cancer had killed her within four months. There had been tears and anger at the end, especially from Dad, who had seethed from the injustice of his wife taken too soon.

If Ben believed in a god he'd have raged against it until his lungs burned.

He stayed by the grave until the sky clouded, threaded with black and grey clotting over the sun. He said a few words to her then rose from the graveside, easing his stiffened joints with cold fingers. He walked back up the slope to where the path was cracked and cold. He pulled up his jacket collar against the dropping temperature.

A tall, stoop-shouldered man stood under one of the trees by the pathway, his back turned to Ben, dressed in a brown raincoat. From the raising of his hand to his face he looked to be wiping his mouth and removing something unsavoury from his lips. The man made no sound as he dwelled in the damp grass under the tree, shadowed by the thick bough of pine.

Ben had a sudden irrational fear of seeing the man's face; that it wouldn't be a kind face but something cruel and awful instead. He approached the tall man and coughed to clear his throat. Like an animal disturbed during feeding, the man stopped wiping his mouth and looked up.

Ben halted on the path.

The man turned. Large bovine eyes startled with surprise. A pale face, all severe angles and skin pulled tight across bone. His mouth opened without words. A clerical collar around his neck. Holy man. A shaman with neatly-combed, oil-slicked hair. Shoes polished but wet and covered with grass clippings.

"Are you okay?" Ben said.

The man ran a hand over his face and looked at his feet, then back at Ben, and he nodded, some colour blooming in his sallow cheeks. He stepped onto the pathway and put his hands in the pockets of his coat.

"Yes, thank you. I was just thinking of something. Time ran away from me."

"Must have been some pretty deep thoughts," said Ben.

The man gave a nervous smile. His nostrils were pink and moist, exhaling damply like livestock. "It would seem so." His accent was pure Home Counties. Ben imagined the man sat in a drawing room reading leather-bound books and sipping tea from a bone china cup.

"I don't know you, do I?" the man said. "Do you live locally? I've never seen you around here, and I don't forget a face." Despite being spoken softly, the words seemed like a challenge or a gentle interrogation.

"I've just moved back for a while. I was born in the village; lived here until I was twenty-four. Do you know Victor Ottway?"

"Victor?" the man said, with the sloped crook of a smile in his face. "Yes, I know Victor very well. He attends the service every Sunday." The man paused, sniffed and dabbed at his nose with a tissue from his pocket. "You must be Ben."

"Uh, yeah."

The man loped over in one long stride and grasped Ben's hand, shook it lightly with delicate fingers, then let go slowly. "Your father speaks very highly of you."

"Really?"

"So sorry about your mother. I understand she was a lovely woman. A great loss to the village. Victor has talked about her, too. My predecessor, Reverend Finch, officiated at her funeral, if I remember correctly."

"That's right," Ben said. "When did Reverend Finch leave?"

"Last year. He had terrible trouble with his heart."

"He died?"

"No, but he suffered two heart attacks in six months, so he was retired from service. I was asked to replace him." The man shook his head. "I'm sorry, where are my manners? I'm Reverend Mark Glass. Pleased to meet you."

Ben nodded, his arms dangling and feeling useless at his sides. He shifted awkwardly on his feet.

Glass said, "I'm sorry about your wife. Victor told me. Such an awful thing to happen."

"She isn't dead," Ben said.

Glass nodded, one side of his mouth curling slightly. His eyes flicked over Ben's right shoulder and Ben had the sudden feeling someone was creeping up behind him. Crows cried overhead and cast flittering shadows on the ground. Glass looked up at the birds and frowned.

"For how long are you back, Ben?"

"A few weeks. Maybe longer. I'm thinking of moving back down here for good."

"From Shrewsbury?" Glass said. Dad seemed to have told the reverend everything about him.

"Yes."

Glass bunched his hands together. Toothy smile and blunt incisors. Frail chin. "I'm sure your father would love to have you back in the village permanently. I get the impression that he's very lonely. Nobody should be lonely. Don't you agree?"

Ben hesitated. "Unless they want to be."

Glass nodded. "Of course. We are our own masters."

Ben wasn't sure what he meant by that. "I suppose so."

"Indeed." Glass rolled up his sleeve and checked his watch. He coughed wetly into a cupped hand. "Well, I must be on my way. I have parish paperwork to attend and it won't do itself. It's not as glamorous as it sounds."

Ben forced a smile. "I'm sure it isn't."

"Pleased to meet you." Glass offered his hand and they shook again.

"You too, Reverend."

"Maybe I'll see you here with your father on Sunday. I think he'd like that."

"Maybe," Ben said.

Glass smiled and walked away towards the church entrance. Ben walked in the opposite direction and pulled his jacket tighter around his chest.

The only way they'd get him into a church was if they shackled him in iron chains and dragged him there.

Three

Ben walked the streets and lanes of Marchwood till late afternoon. He visited his old haunts and half-remembered places.

His old friends were gone and nothing was the same. They had escaped the fugue and slow decay of the village, the deep cold and the iron ground. But now he was back here, grounded, his wings clipped. He found it hard to make friends and even harder to keep them. Personality defects and a penchant for over-examining things were not endearing traits. There was a knot of darkness in his heart. Something malfunctioning in his brain. Maybe Emily really did leave him, after all. Maybe she didn't just vanish into the wind.

There could have been another man. Someone better than him.

~

He returned to his father's house as the light faded and the pallid moon rose. Dad was in his armchair watching an old war film.

"Have you eaten yet?" Ben asked him.

Dad shook his head and raised his whiskey glass.

Ben went into the kitchen and scratched together

a meal of chicken soup and cheese crackers. They ate in silence and watched Richard Burton and Clint Eastwood in *Where Eagles Dare*.

After dinner, Dad broke out cans of lager. Ben drank until the room began to melt around him.

~

He sees the dark between worlds. The cosmic trenches. Terrible things dwell within those abyssal canyons.

He watched the revolution of galaxies and fading suns. Cold enough to stop your heart and turn your breath to black ice. The song of the stars in his mind. Alien colours behind his eyes. An open door. A whisper across eons and realities.

The lights are extinguished until there are none left.

~

Ben woke in pitch black, terrified he had lost his sight during sleep. The lunatic rhythm of his heart in his chest. Idiot fear. The sweat from his skin had dampened the sheets underneath him.

His bed. His bedroom. He pawed for the lamp at his side. The sudden light stung his eyes but calmed his heart. There was no spit in his mouth and he wriggled his tongue over his gums and furred teeth. The room dipped and swayed, spun around him until his guts climbed into his chest, and he had to sit on the edge of the bed and hold his head in his hands.

He looked up, groaning into his palms, and peered over the tips of his fingers. The light from the landing slipped under the bottom of his door.

Ben shrugged on a t-shirt from the floor and traipsed onto the landing, placing his palms against the walls to stay upright. The floor seemed to undulate. He shook his head. The light was too bright and he covered his eyes with one hand. Dad's bedroom door was open. Ben entered. Empty bed and ruffled sheets. Bad breath and stale alcohol in the air.

He headed downstairs. The hairs on the backs of his legs pricked up. The living room light was on, but the room was empty. He shivered as a cold breeze came in from the kitchen. The lights were on in there too.

Ben moved slowly, chewing the inside of his mouth, his hands by his thighs. He breathed in, smelled the chill night air and grass damp with dew.

The kitchen floor was cold under his bare feet. His father stood in the front doorway, trembling, facing the darkness beyond the garden and dressed only in his underwear. Stooped spine. His skin was pale enough to be that of a corpse. His fingers curled and uncurled at his sides, over and over. He made no sound.

"Dad?" Ben said, his voice throaty and dry and much too loud. His father didn't answer, nor turn to acknowledge him. He took hold of Dad's cold shoulders and pulled him back from the doorway.

Dad let himself be moved, limbs malleable, and he stood unmoving as Ben looked out at the night and the dark houses full of dreamers.

The sky was full of stars. Fluctuating colours and cold light. He closed the door, locked it, and turned back to his father.

Dad's breaths came slowly, pulled from his lungs, and his body shook and cringed, wasted muscles gnarled and bunched into weak knots. Tears in his eyes. A weeping mouth. Ben wiped his father's face with a damp tea towel.

His father's eyes widened and his mouth fell open. "What's going on, Ben? What're you doing?"

"I found you standing in the doorway," Ben said. "Are you okay? What happened?"

His father looked up, with eyes rimmed pink and bloodshot, mouth twitching. His voice came out on glass. "I dunno. Fell asleep. Uh, don't remember. Just remember waking up with you wiping my face with a bloody tea towel and freezing my arse off."

"You were looking outside, Dad." Ben kept his voice low.

"Was someone out there?"

"I don't think so. You were sleepwalking."

"Yes." Dad dropped his head.

"You're sure you didn't see anyone?"

"I saw nothing. I'm very tired, Ben."

"Same here." Ben poured a glass of water for his father, took him upstairs and back to bed.

"Thank you," Dad muttered as Ben pulled the sheets up to his chest. "You're a good lad." He took a sip of water then placed it at the bedside.

"No worries, Dad. Get some sleep. Try not to go for a walk until you wake up."

"Cheeky sod."

"Goodnight, Dad."

"Goodnight."

After Ben returned to bed, his last thought before he fell asleep was of an immense carnivorous mouth eating the sky and the stars within.

~

The first light turned black to grey and melted the stars into a weak yellow glow where the curve of the Earth met the sky.

Seated on the wooden bench in the back garden, Ben remembered fragments of his dreams: images of winged spindly creatures soaring over a deserted city of black monoliths; immense membranes that swallowed continents; a sea of boiling froth spewing dead marine life. He sipped coffee from trembling hands and smoked while watching the sun rise. Beyond the garden the scrubland was silent, and the houses further on were dark enough to be considered uninhabited.

Grey-blue smoke seeped from between his teeth and coiled into serpent-shapes. He inhaled and slumped against the bench, his spine aching from a night of restless sleep. The taste of the cigarette covered the stagnant taste in his mouth and greased his teeth with an oily residue he had to wash away with the coffee. His lungs swelled with smoke until he coughed harshly into the cold air.

The patio door opened and his father limped outside, grunting and sniffling in a tattered brown dressing gown and rubbing his eyes with the heels of his hands. He cleared his throat and spat on the lawn.

"How're you feeling, Dad?"

His father sat next to him, groaning as his bones adjusted to new positions. He breathed slowly.

"Like shit through a grinder. Sorry about last night, lad. I don't know what happened."

"No problem," Ben said.

"How much did we drink?"

"Not that much, I think."

"I haven't sleepwalked since I was your age."

"It's fine, Dad. These things happen. The important thing is you're okay."

Dad looked at him then towards the distant houses across from them. "I had a dream last night."

Something twitched in Ben's chest. "Yeah?"

"I was walking through a ruined land. Black towers were all that remained and they loomed over piles of bleached-white bones. Ash blew on a rotting breeze. It was a dead world."

"Sounds fucking horrible."

Dad gave a tragic smile. Ben didn't mention his own dreams or how his brain kept throwing up images of his father feeble with some crippling ailment and steadily growing weaker and more muddled. It was strange that both of them had experienced such vivid, frightening dreams.

Dad nodded at the cigarette. "Let's have one of those."

Ben frowned. "You sure? You gave up years ago."

"I need one after the night I've had. If you don't mind..."

"No problem."

With bony fingers, Dad took a cigarette from the pack. Ben lit it for him, and he sucked on the cigarette until his nose leaked smoke and he coughed harshly and he smacked his chest hard enough to make Ben worry his breastbone might have caved in.

The old man wheezed, glanced at Ben. "I forgot how good they taste."

"Fill your boots." Ben placed the small clay ashtray between them, which he'd made at school as a gift for Dad in the long gone days. He tapped ash from his cigarette into the lumpy, misshapen bowl and noticed small thumbprints imprinted into the hardened clay during its making, a reminder of the boy he was twenty years ago.

They smoked in silence for a while as the houses around them came to life. A dog barked. The chatter of a radio from a neighbour's open window. A toilet flushed. A crying baby. Lazy Saturday morning. A plane flew over at high-altitude, leaving ghost-trails in its wake.

"I spoke to Reverend Glass yesterday," Ben said. "Seems a decent bloke."

"Yeah, he's nice enough."

"I didn't know you'd been attending church."

Dad took a long drag and blew smoke through his nostrils. His fingers twitched. "I started going last year. It helps."

"I didn't think you believed in that stuff."

"I didn't. But things change, lad."

Ben filled his mouth with coffee so he couldn't reply.

"I have to tell myself that your mother's waiting for me, wherever she is. If I didn't believe – if I knew I would never see her again – I don't know what I'd do."

"Don't say that, Dad." He thought about whether he'd ever see Emily again; to never get the chance to look at her face, speak to her and tell her she was loved, turned his guts cold and watery and enclosed his heart in iron.

"Fancy coming with me tomorrow?" Dad said.

Ben's cigarette burned down to the tips of his fingers and he stubbed it out in the ashtray. "I don't know, Dad. Probably not a good idea. I'd catch fire as soon as I walked inside."

"Don't be ridiculous," said Dad. "It doesn't matter if you don't believe."

"But isn't that the whole point of going to church?"

"I don't care. I'd just like you to come with me. Just this once."

"Don't try to convert me, Dad."

"Don't be stupid. It's not about that; it's about keeping your old man company."

"I'll think about it."

"Good lad."

The sun rose in yellow and red, and painted the horizon with fire.

~

Ben walked the fields and wide open spaces in the washed out light of winter. The fields were soaked in shades of iron and the scarred ground was hardened by cold wind. The branches of crooked trees creaked and swayed, and the yellowed grass stirred around his feet. The sky was moving.

He stood on the hillside and looked down at Marchwood, a clot of autumnal brown and wet wood among ashen land and earth. The church steeple loomed above the houses in the centre of the village, a reminder of the old ways. The recreation ground, where the football and cricket teams played, was at the north end of the village. It was a swathe of dark green bordered by horse chestnut trees and thin dirt lanes. He could see the goalposts, the pavilion and the fenced off cricket pitch.

Beyond the village were harvested fields stubbled with spikes of corn. Scrubland and frozen earth, hedgerows and thickets of hawthorn and blackberry bushes. A thin plume of smoke rose from a farmhouse chimney. Chicken wire fences held up by lichen-stained wooden posts. Galvanised steel gates to let livestock in and out of the fields. Dark trees huddled in groves, scraped bare by winter. The abandoned caravan park a mile outside the village was like a haunted place of cardboard ghosts and mildewed desolation. Near the apple orchard to the east of the village was a wood of oaks and willows, where shadows spilled from between the tall trees and birds chittered unseen. In his youth he had built dens and ramshackle treehouses there with his friends. He used to come home to his parents with his hands covered in scratches and sticky with sap.

He raised his father's binoculars to his face and

watched crows alight on spindly tree branches and tend to their nests. A kestrel flitted over a field, scanning the ground for tiny mammals. In one of the distant fields a herd of deer were grazing beneath the shelter of birches and elms. In other directions were the dense stains of other villages and towns.

He walked on, skirting around patches of thick mud and dull puddles, followed by the ambient noise of wildlife, the whispered breeze and the shifting of the land. Small creatures darted through hedgerows. A pheasant's idiot call startled him as he passed a small skeletal grove of stunted birches.

Ben found the remains of a fox in one field, and he was caught between sadness and fascination. Bone and tufts of reddish hair. The grin of a curved jaw. Dulled teeth grimed with black decay. The bones had been scattered by scavengers.

In the end, everything returned to the earth. Ben was vaguely comforted by the thought.

He passed through a meadow of long grass. Mice fled from his heavy feet. An adder slipped away into forests of yellowed stems. His jeans were wet up to his knees when he emerged.

Small lanes snaked through the fields and pastures. A herd of cows watched him when he passed. He thought he saw a short, slight figure moving among the herd, but when he looked again no one was there and he was faced only with vacant, bovine stares, chewing mouths and the pungent stench of ripe, steaming dung.

He rubbed his head against the dull ache of a migraine. He was starting to flag, his legs prickling and stiff, each breath taken too quickly and stinging in his lungs. A stitch in one side. His stomach muscles cramped. He stopped and hunched over towards the patchy grass and scrub. It was all downhill after his best years; muscles grew weaker and took longer to recover, parts of the body that had once been lean and firm became so much fatty soft tissue. He'd regret the walk when he woke tomorrow morning.

He was about to turn back towards the village when he paused, sure he had heard someone say his name. But when he looked around, there was just a low wind slipping across the fields. He shut his eyes against the pain inside his skull, and when he opened them his vision blurred at the edges and a metallic ringing steadily grew louder until it seemed that its source was on top of him. He bent over with his hands on his thighs and tried to spit the taste of chemicals from his mouth.

And now other sounds were coming through. Growing louder and nearer. Animal sounds. The songs of dying marine mammals caught in nets. Keening wails and lamenting cries from cavernous lungs. Barks and yips of creatures he hadn't heard before; the cacophony of an alien forest.

Ben clasped his hands to his ears. The sounds came at him from all directions and the ringing was like glass in his eardrums, and that was when he felt the heat of being watched from hidden places around him. Something closing in. Electric ghosts inside his skull. He covered his face, and when he raised his head to look at the sky it was violent with thrashing waves and squalls; an impossible thing for the sky to be, a silent storm raging on another world.

His legs gave way, knees buckling, and he fell to the cold dirt, reduced to instinct and fear and the white terror of prey animals. But he was mesmerised by the impossible sky; it had lost its violence and was now composed of alien hues and shades twisting and entwining. He tried to speak, but his breath was stolen and his lungs were flat and crumpled like a punctured balloon.

His eyes were watering. He didn't touch the tears in case they were the colour of ruptured things and internal bleeding. He gritted his teeth and cried. The sky, the ringing and the animal sounds wiped away all cognitive thought and left him open-mouthed and breathless. If this was the light show at the end of his life, the farewell for failing synapses and degrading neurons, he didn't want to die screaming and shitting. Time blurred and ran like melting wax. Movement in the treeline. The grind of the earth underneath him. A harsh laugh that wasn't from a human mouth.

He curled into a foetal shape and shut his eyes against a sky drowning in black stars. Bleeding voids were flash-burned into his mind. He was nothing but a pounding heart wrapped in skin and flesh.

Ben wept into his hands and cried for his lost wife.

Four

He dreams, and he knows he is dreaming, but the fear creeping up his spine and into his brain stem is real enough. He can't feel his heart; it is a silent muscle and the rush of his blood is slow and weak. He is too scared to move, lost and abandoned in howling darkness.

He is being scrutinized by intelligences far beyond his ape-like grasp. He is an insect to them, a worm, a cockroach – a fragile, irrational suit of bones and meat barely surviving on the lowest reaches of the evolutionary ladder. He is fodder. And he screams when the darkness pours over his tender skin.

~

Ben came to in the dead silence with soil in his hair and dried tears under his eyes. For a terrifying moment his mind was blank, but then images and names returned to him, and he remembered his name as he dug fingernails into his palms so that he didn't forget again.

He stared at the sky and it was grey and still, a sky he recognised. Rain speckled his face. His eyelids were heavy and all he wanted to do was sleep until the end of winter.

Shapes stood over him. One was tall, the other

short and low to the ground. The short one had bad breath and licked at his fingers. The tall one said something, but Ben couldn't hear it because his ears felt like they were swaddled with cloth.

He sighed and passed out again.

~

He woke stretched upon a crumpled sofa in a room revealed by insipid light and the flickering glow of a black and white portable television. He rubbed his eyes, swallowing down a dry and swollen throat, and groaned at the leaden beat of dull pain spreading through his brow. His limbs were heavy and his stomach felt like it had been emptied and then refilled with straw and burlap. He sat up and cradled his head until the pain throbbing against the walls of his skull lessened to something tolerable.

The room smelled of dust and reminded him of his granddad's shed he used to sneak into and gawp at the spiders' nests and webs that covered the ceiling.

He glimpsed a patch of ashen sky beyond the window. There was a lone door with flaking red paint and a rusted brass handle. One side of the room was heaped with stacks of old books, yellowed sheets of paper and leather-bound photo albums. Next to the sofa, a glass of water and a plate of sandwiches had been left upon a small pine table.

Despite his thirst, he didn't touch the water. The sandwiches were thin slices of white bread cut into two halves; his stomach lurched at the sight of pale green lettuce and limp cuts of grey meat within.

On the wall opposite was a large canvas painting of arboreal primates with doll faces, cavorting in spiked black trees set against red mountains. His flesh crawled at those sullen, black-eyed masks. The creatures' limbs were too gangly and thin to be useful for scaling branches, and the flickering of the television gave the primates the illusion of movement. For a moment he thought several of them turned to look at him, and he couldn't study it for more than a few seconds before he had to avert his eyes and look at something more mundane like the wooden floorboards or the bare walls of cracked plaster.

He was relieved to find his wallet, keys, mobile phone, cigarettes and lighter still in his pockets. He checked the mobile: no messages or missed calls. For almost two hours he'd been unconscious.

When he stood, holding out his arms to his sides, the room swayed. He went to the window and looked out at a wide garden of tangled brush, weeds and an ancient pond choked with thick algae. Beyond that was an empty swimming pool, its insides stained with streaks of brown-red rust.

From deeper in the house behind him, he heard

music muffled by the closed door. Industrial ambient-metal. Slow percussion of metal drums. Droning electronics like a cosmic transmission. Distorted notes from a synthesizer. The sounds of hammers upon granite and pickaxes gouging at a mine face. Sounds of iron and mechanical limbs. Choking furnaces.

Ben opened the door and stepped into a hallway with a stairway to his left leading up to a darkened landing where shadows crawled over the walls. The music was louder. Bare floorboards. Dust ingrained into the wood. The smell of old things. He chose not to climb the steps. Along the corridor was a door set into the wall on his right. He put his ear to the door and listened. Hard to tell if anyone was in there, due to the music drifting down the corridor. He tried the handle, but it only twisted so far and the door wouldn't give.

He swallowed a lump in his throat and followed the music into a large room at the end of the corridor, where the walls were covered in watercolour paintings that depicted unsettling things with bulging eyes and a myriad of limbs.

Ben stood in the middle of the windowless room and spun slowly. The music was pulsing and pounding, filling his head. Horrors on the walls: a wide red mouth where a nest of tongues writhed; the fossilized remains of a leviathan-like creature embedded in the dust basin of a dried up lake; a bulbous mass of white flesh, a sagging sow, with newborns sucking eagerly from its pink teats.

There were also charcoal illustrations of hooked appendages, alien ligaments and nervous systems. A tall figure with a pallid yellow mask. Things with thrashing tendrils and black wings. A horned titan rising from a boiling lake. Insectile facades and crab-like monsters pawing pale meat into their craws. Anatomical sketches of animals from a lost age: flightless giant birds, tusked predators and serpentine beasts. The last painting he viewed, before he lowered his face towards the floor and fought the urge to scratch at his eyes, showed him giant worms with snapping lamprey mouths erupting from oceanic trenches.

There was a door at the far end of the room, and the music was behind it.

~

Ben opened the door into a wall of noise. Sharp pain flashed across his skull, pulsing in time with his heartbeat. He shut his eyes until the pain passed, then entered the room. Tucked away in a shadowed corner, away from the watery light slipping through the bay window, a tall man hunched over a mounted canvas, swigging from a can of Red Bull. The smell of paint and turpentine filled the dense air. Ben took a step towards him before he noticed the Irish wolfhound by the man's feet and halted. The dog unfolded from the floor and stared at him. Its dark eyes centred upon Ben and its mouth opened just enough to reveal mottled pink-black gums and large teeth the colour of ivory.

Alerted by the dog's movement, the man turned to face Ben. There was a dark doorway behind him. He was gaunt and shaven-headed, a reddish beard down to his chest where it had been woven into two long plaits. Reddened blemishes under his eyes. He wore a white apron stained with all colours of paint, but dominated by red, and it gave him the appearance of a butcher fresh from gutting farm animals. His arms were bare and heavily tattooed with runic patterns, pagan symbols and coiled serpents. He wore combat trousers and heavy boots.

Ben stepped back.

The man reached over to the table next to him and turned off the stereo. In the silence Ben tried to speak but his breath caught in his throat. The tattooed man placed his paintbrush in a jar. The colours ran like blood in water.

"Finally," the man said. "I was worried you wouldn't wake up." His voice was low and cheerless. "I made you some sandwiches." He finished his drink, crushed the can in his hand, and tossed it into a metal bin filled to the top with other empties.

"What happened?" Ben asked. "Where am I?"

The man tucked his hands into the front pockets of his apron. "How are you feeling, Ben?"

"How do you know my name?"

"I checked your wallet and driving license. Do you want to sit down?"

"I want to know what happened." The muscles in Ben's back tensed. His heart pounded too hard. He put one hand to his face and rubbed between his eyes as a needling pain appeared behind them.

"I'll make you a cup of tea." The man gestured towards two dusty armchairs to Ben's right. "Take a seat. Best to take the weight off your feet; you've had a nasty episode. I'll see if there's any cake."

Ben said nothing as the man disappeared through the doorway at the end of the room. The dog remained in place, watching him.

He took a seat.

~

Ben sipped tea between glances at the man who sat opposite him cradling a chipped white mug in calloused hands. They were the hands of a building site labourer or a carpenter, not an artist. The dog lay by his feet, head rested on large paws, eyes closed.

"How's the tea?" the man asked.

"Good." Actually it was bitter and tepid, but the lie was easy.

"I'm Doyle, by the way. Pleased to meet you." He offered a hand. Ben looked at it, hesitated, and then took it in a shaky, clammy grip.

"What happened to me?" Ben asked.

"What do you remember?"

"Not much. I was out walking in the fields. I remember lying on the ground and looking above me. There was something wrong with the sky."

"I found you passed out in a field while I was out taking Fenrir for a walk. I thought you were dead at first. I managed to wake you up enough to get you on your feet. You were feverish, muttering about colours and animal sounds. I brought you back here."

Heat flushed in Ben's face. With a shudder, he recalled looking at the alien sky. That impossible sky.

"Thank you for helping me." Ben felt overwhelmed, unable to grasp what had happened to him. Apart from the incident that initiated his nervous breakdown, he'd never suffered anything similar. No seizures, panic attacks or bouts of fainting. Nothing. Maybe it was because he'd mixed his medication with alcohol. But surely that wouldn't amount to visions of the sky awash with alien storms? Maybe it was something left over from his breakdown, like a forgotten wound opening again.

What if it was a brain tumour? The possibility turned his insides into cold slurry. The prospect of cancer, the illness that had taken his mother, was more terrifying than any mental illness he could imagine. There would be blood tests and meetings with sober-faced, sympathetic physicians. CT scans and chemo. His heart shivered.

Fuck.

"Why didn't you call an ambulance?" Ben said.

Doyle wiped his mouth. "Didn't feel the need. You were fine once I got you back here and laid you on the sofa."

"But what if something had happened to me while I was passed out?"

Doyle shrugged. "But nothing did happen to you. You're fine."

"Hopefully."

"Relax," said Doyle. "Could have been a lot worse."

"I suppose." Ben sipped the last dregs of his now-lukewarm tea. "Are we in Marchwood?"

"Just outside the village. This used to be my parents' house before they moved away a few years ago. Are you from the village?"

"Yeah, grew up there, but moved away. I'm visiting."

"Not the happiest of returns so far," said Doyle.

Ben nodded, worked his jaw and listened to the mandibles crunch like gristle. In the awkward silence he could hear his body creak and groan. He felt old and dry like scraps of leather and bone in a casket. He looked at the walls and the strange images upon them.

"Interesting paintings," he said.

Doyle put down his mug. "I paint my dreams of gods and monsters."

"You see these things in your dreams?"

The grey light darkened Doyle's eyes. He nodded and scratched at his long beard. "Have you had bad dreams?"

"Just normal stuff, I suppose. I've had a rough time in the past few months. Had a lot to deal with."

"What do you dream about? Other worlds? Places you've never seen before?"

"I don't know. What does it matter? Dreams are just dreams." Ben looked to the window; the light was leaving the sky.

Doyle switched on a standing lamp then gestured towards the dog at his feet. "Old Fenrir here is dreaming. I wonder what he's dreaming about. Do you think his dreams are similar to ours, or are they just flashes of colour, light and darkness? Sound and fury." He exhaled, rubbed the corners of his eyes. "I hope he doesn't see the things I've seen."

"I'm sure he just dreams about chasing rabbits," said Ben.

"He doesn't deserve bad dreams." Doyle lowered his face and stroked the hair around his mouth.

"I better get going," said Ben.

Doyle looked up, startled from a thought. "Are you sure you want to cross the fields in the dark?"

Ben rose from the armchair. "I'll be fine, thanks." He hesitated. "I can't thank you enough for helping me, Doyle. I dread to think what might have happened if you hadn't found me."

Doyle stood and stepped over the sleeping dog. They shook hands again. "No problem," Doyle said. "I may see you around sometime." He strode over to a desk of drawers, and when he returned he thrust a torch into Ben's hand.

"I can make my way home without that," Ben said.

"Just take it," said Doyle. "Darkness falls sooner than you think out there."

"Very generous of you."

"No problem. I'll show you out."

They left the room. Ben made sure not to look back at the gods and monsters that covered the walls.

Five

The gloom of the fields was becoming night and deep shadow. Hillside thickets like oil stains. He walked across the fields towards the village, the torch beam cutting the dark ahead but doing little to push it from his path. No stars above, the sky impenetrable, black and low.

The streetlights of Marchwood showed him the way home, and he could discern the location of his father's house. It gave him comfort and quickened his step. He'd been walking for ten minutes, ignoring the suggestions of movement to his flanks and the muffled slap of footfalls keeping their distance behind him. He tripped and stumbled on small mounds of hard earth and jagged stones. Adrenaline churned his stomach.

One foot in front of the other. Sweat like chip grease on his face; he licked his lips, tasted it, and spat into the gloom.

A fox barked from across the fields. The whisper of swaying tree branches. A shape bolted through a hedgerow. On the shallow slope far on his left, something grey and barely visible dashed out of sight.

Don't stop. Don't look.

The torch shook in his slickened grip; the light

skittered and bobbed like something trying to escape him. The dark closed in, touched his shoulders and stroked the skin of his face. He breathed hard, trying not to hyperventilate, to calm the motion of his chest. Childhood terrors rushed back to him. The nape of his neck tingled. Traces of genetic heritage, fuelled by the fear of the dark and the predators that preyed on early humans. That fear, honed by evolution and the deaths of millions, but dulled by the indolent lifestyle of the modern world, had never left Man.

And then he was out of the fields and into the narrow, muddy lanes leading into the village. Someone was keeping pace with him in the field to his right, moving behind the trees.

The first streetlight was almost fifty yards ahead. Nearly there. He blinked sweat from his eyes and the cold air dried the drips that beaded on his face.

He reached the streetlight and paused in its glow, then turned back to look at the darkness and it seemed to swell and rise like a black tide of oil.

In the low clouds, there was thunder.

~

The streets were quiet and empty except for the occasional car passing by and two youths in hoodies loitering outside a house, passing a cigarette between themselves. The dancing glow of televisions behind curtains drawn against the night. The rich smells of dinners cooking in kitchens. A dog barked from a nearby back yard. A storm was building, pumping itself up like a boxer ready to fight, and there were already flecks of rain in the scuttling wind that pulled at Ben's body.

He reached his father's house just as the rain came down. A faint light from the kitchen window. And when Ben entered the house, Dad was asleep and slumped in his armchair like a boneless thing, draped in the dressing gown he'd worn that morning. Empty lager cans and a plate of congealed baked beans on the floor by his feet. The musty smell reminded Ben of toiling among the tables at a jumble sale. There were mystery stains on the breast of his father's dressing gown.

Dad had been sat there all day.

The television showed a breaking story on the BBC News. A female reporter outside a primary school in Crouch End, London. Squad cars and ambulances. Police vans. Flashing blue lights and umbrellas in the rain.

Ben dropped onto the sofa. The unusual events of the day were forgotten as he stared at the television screen.

"The unidentified man entered the school with a shotgun just before midday and opened fire upon the first class of children he found. Then he proceeded to walk the

corridors for the next fifteen minutes, shooting at anyone he encountered. Then he went outside to engage the police armed response units and was killed by three shots to the chest. Four teachers and eight children were killed; five children were injured and taken to hospital."

"Jesus," Ben muttered, his face numb and cold, the blood gone from his hands. Photos of the children appeared on the screen. Smiling boys and girls never to smile again.

Ben switched off the television, unable to look any longer at the faces of dead kids.

In the silence of the house he listened to the rain falling outside the four walls and closed his eyes against rising despair for his species.

~

The following morning came in weak light and heavy rain that had poured all night and soaked the ground.

Ben felt glum and lethargic from troubled sleep and bad dreams he could barely remember. He took his medication then chased it with two aspirin he swallowed with a gulp of coffee. His guts slurped and jittered, and his back was a puzzle of painful knots that punished him with jabbing fingers to his spine whenever he tried to move. His 'episode' in the fields, coupled with the news of the school shooting in Crouch End, left him shocked, sick and appalled. He thought about the parents of the children, and those children and teachers who had survived, left to pick through the aftermath. Their futures would be filled with funerals.

His father was in the kitchen, hunched over the cooker, nodding his head to the Sex Pistols. Ben sat at the dining table and chewed on a bowl of cornflakes. He'd turned down Dad's offer of bacon, eggs, sausages, baked beans and black pudding. His stomach was fragile, like liquid in a plastic bag.

Dad dished up the greasy contents of the frying pan. Ben's guts twinged. Dad sat down opposite him and began snaffling up slippery bacon and cuts of sausage into his mouth.

Ben blew air between his teeth and watched as the middle parts of his body cramped.

"Did you have a good walk yesterday?" Dad asked him.

"Yeah, fine." There was no point mentioning what had happened in the fields. No point in worrying his father with something that might have been a one-off.

"Where did you go?"

"Just around the fields. Nothing too exerting."

His father eyed him. "What else?"

"What do you mean?"

"You're holding something back, lad. I could always read you."

Ben hesitated, pushed away his bowl of damp cornflakes. "I met a man out in the fields."

Dad raised his eyebrows. "Really? Something you want to tell me? You starting to swing the other way now, lad?"

"Shut up, Dad."

"Only having a joke."

"Not funny."

Dad sighed. "Continue."

"His name was Doyle. Bit of an eccentric bloke but nice enough."

"Doyle?" Dad said. "Tall man with a long beard and a shaven head? Looked like he needs a good meal? Had an Irish wolfhound?"

"Do you know him?"

"Best to stay away from him."

"Why?"

"Bit of an oddball. A loner. He's well-known around the village. He used to be in the army."

"Really?"

"Apparently he was discharged because of mental problems. Caused some trouble. Done some bad things, I'd heard."

"What did he do?"

"I've only heard rumours."

"About what?"

"I don't know for sure. Something about him being involved in an accident. Other soldiers died. That sort of stuff."

"Fucking hell."

"I know."

"He seemed alright."

"I wouldn't trust him." Dad guzzled from his cup of tea. "Still want to come with me to church today?"

"Oh shit, I forgot."

"You don't have to come. I just thought it'd be nice. Especially with what happened to those children in London."

Ben frowned.

"It's up to you, lad."

"If you want me to come with you, Dad..."

"Only if you don't mind. Don't want to force anything upon you or be a nuisance."

"I'll come along, Dad. It's not a nuisance. There's no danger of me being converted."

"Jesus loves you," Dad said, and smiled thinly through a mouthful of meat.

~

The smell of incense and damp clothes, foot powder and ointment. Candlelight in far corners of old wood and ancient stone constructed by men now long-dead. People were seated in the rows of pews separated by a narrow aisle. Hard rain against the stained glass windows, and water dripped into a tin bucket from a leak in the roof where the wooden rafters were dark, thick and gnarled in the high ceiling.

Reverend Glass, thin and bird-like while ensconced in the pulpit, spoke in reserved tones through a mouth that barely moved. His voice echoed around the stone walls. His eyes flitted over the sparse congregation, his flock. After Glass had opened the service with a prayer for the dead schoolchildren in Crouch End, Ben had tuned out everything else and passed the time by observing the rest of the congregation while chewing on the inside of his mouth. They were mainly old people in their Sunday best, mainly alone and clinging to old beliefs, unable to face death without the emotional salve of a benevolent god and an afterlife filled with loved ones and dead pets. Widows and widowers wringing their hands, hunched over and crooked on the creaking pews, their eyes set upon Reverend Glass and following the movements of his bony hands.

The parishioners looked tired and jaded, sallow faces white and grey and worn into dull edges. Old women with wispy hair, their faces painted with thick make-up, their handkerchiefs wiping at dry eyes. Sniffles and knotted shoulders. Hunched spinsters and pot-bellied widowers. Balding scalps and white hair. The smell of shoe polish and moth balls.

There was desperation here, so thick in the air that it left a layer of grease on the skin. These people were terrified of oblivion and whatever came after that final heartbeat. Terrified of not knowing.

Aren't we all?

Ben didn't think that oblivion would be such a bad thing, if it was all that waited after death. No pain, no fear, no more problems, the end of heartache and worrying. No more waking up in the middle of the night reaching for Emily, only to realise she wasn't there.

In the really dark hours, in the house they had shared together, he often contemplated the positives of suicide, but despite this he had no urge to kill himself; he lacked the constitution. Sometimes he wished he didn't. Sometimes he wished he was a braver man.

Next to Ben, Dad sat with his hands worrying at the hymn book on his lap, his face loose and clammy. He was clad in an ill-fitting navy blue suit too large for his scrawny body. Ben hadn't seen him wear a suit since Mum's funeral.

Dad was hanging on the reverend's every word, papery lips partly open, a bead of sweat sliding down his face. He muttered something under his breath but Ben couldn't discern it. High in the rafters, Ben heard a fluttering of wings. He looked up sharply, but saw nothing. No birds or bats. Patches of shadow. No movement up there high above the faithful.

To his left an old woman was wiping her mouth with a sodden tissue. She turned to Ben with glazed eyes circled by sandpaper skin. She smiled at him, damp-mouthed and toothless, then raised a liver-spotted hand and waved slowly at him, and he could only nod at her and smile politely when all he wanted to do was cover his eyes so he didn't have to look at her any longer.

The woman turned away to watch Reverend Glass, her hands set primly on her lap.

The next hymn was announced. *All Things Bright and Beautiful*. The congregation rose, grating and grimacing, laboured breaths and winces drawn from the bending of joints and ligaments.

Ben helped his father stand. The hymn started with the muddled piping of the organ. Air drawn into dusty lungs. Murmured lyrics.

Ben didn't sing.

~

After the service, the congregation exited the church in a slow procession of trembling legs, walking sticks and shuffling feet. A little boy asked his mother if Jesus had a pet dragon, and she chastised him. Reverend Glass stood by the door on their way out and bid farewell to each person, smiling wetly through a glazed mouth and too many teeth. Dad told Glass he had enjoyed the service.

Ben shook the reverend's hand and it was warm, clammy and moist like mushroom flesh. Glass smiled at him and one corner of the reverend's mouth trembled and faltered. He smelled of aniseed. Ben let go of his hand and moved on.

The rest of the congregation melted away into the rain like ghosts going home.

Driving back through the village, Ben pulled over to let another car through a narrow section of road. A shadow passed over them, moving fast, a flicker of spiked darkness. When he looked up he saw nothing but the rain and black sky.

"What was that?" Ben said.

"What was what?" said Dad, staring out the window at the houses.

Ben watched the sky but whatever it had been was gone. "Doesn't matter," he said and drove on.

When they arrived home there was an ambulance outside a neighbour's house up the road. Ben parked the car and they stepped out, pulling their hoods up against the rain.

A small crowd had gathered near the ambulance. Blank faces in the downpour. Two paramedics wheeled out a man on a gurney, an oxygen mask over his face like an octopoid thing, trailed by his wife and son, who were hunched over against the downpour. The paramedics hauled the man into the ambulance and closed the doors.

The ambulance drove away, blue lights flashing. The man's wife and son followed by car.

The crowd dispersed while the siren pierced the falling rain.

Six

It had been raining for two days straight, with no sign of it abating. Ben had stayed inside since leaving the church service on Sunday, having no wish or inclination to leave the house. His father stayed in bed for long periods. Time seemed to pass like a dream. He kept away from alcohol and the empty promises it made to him of solace and warmth. Meals were eaten and forgotten, although he tried to eat sparingly so he could savour the coiled hunger in his gut. He ran his hands over the walls and felt the bricks beneath the wallpaper and plaster. On the stairway walls he found dark finger smudges from his boyhood.

Standing before the open fridge, he surveyed a roast chicken carcass that was mostly bone and scraps of pale flesh upon a dinner plate. It smelled awful, so he threw it in the bin.

He dreamed of giant stars consuming ashen planets in a time when the Earth was young and lifeless; of ringed moons and gas giants, interstellar concussions lost in deep time and the boiling oceans of alien worlds.

He spent hours stood in the back doorway, chain-smoking and watching the rain. He fretted about seeing a doctor regarding his collapse in the fields, but eventually decided against it, worried that he would have to talk about his breakdown and the events that preceded it. He brooded over Emily and wondered if it was raining wherever she was right now, dead or alive. He wondered if her bones were wet.

He whiled away an afternoon going through Mum's old photo albums. Different generations of the family. Polaroid memories. Photos of Ben as a little boy playing football with Dad or reading a book of nursery rhymes with his mother. Some of the photos showed his parents in their best years, young and happy, full of laughter, a long while before the waning of immune systems and encroachment of disease.

A photo of Ben as a baby on the beach at Weymouth, head sheltered from the sun by a floppy hat, staring at a dead crab Dad had plucked from the shallows. Another shot from the same day: mother feeding him ice cream, and the look of genuine love and affection on her face almost broke his heart.

There were pages dedicated to long-dead relatives; uncles and aunts, a cousin who had died tragically young. Family pets from long ago. He ran one finger over a photo of Dad's old dog Stumpy, a black and white collie that had died two days before Ben's sixteenth birthday.

By the time Ben had finished with the albums, his eyes were damp and aching.

His mobile started beeping. He took it out of his pocket. He didn't recognise the number. The only person who called him these days was Dad, but the old man was downstairs sleeping off half a bottle of whiskey.

Ben answered. "Hello?"

A delay. Low breathing. The faint sound of rain and wind.

"Hello?" he repeated.

"*Ben,*" a voice said. A familiar voice.

"Who's this?"

"*It's Doyle.*"

Ben was caught off guard, and he had to wet his mouth so he could speak. "Doyle? How did you get my number?"

"*I took it from your phone. When you were passed out at my house.*"

"You think it's okay to do something like that?"

"*I took your number because I knew I'd need to call you eventually.*"

"What do you want, Doyle?"

Rain hissed down the line. "*Meet me at the caravan park. I've found something you won't believe.*"

~

The tall gates of the caravan park were chained and

padlocked, rattling in the wind that swept, whistled and swooped. Ben waited in the car while the rain drew ringlets against the windscreen and the engine cooled to the tick of his heart. His fingers gripped the ignition keys; it would only take one slow turn of his hand and he could leave this wretched place behind. It was all painted in dismal, despondent shades of rust and desolation. A place people had gone when they wanted to die.

I'll meet you inside the park, Doyle had said. *I'll find you.*

At the back of his mind, a little voice whispered suggestions that Doyle had lured him out here for reasons he wouldn't discover until it was too late and he was trussed up and ready for butchering. The skin on his arms prickled and his mouth tasted like sour milk as he recalled his father's warning. His heart was quick and his stomach uneasy.

So why had he come out here?

Because Doyle had helped him, and he felt he owed the man something for that, even if it was just an hour of his time and some patience.

He withdrew the keys from the ignition and exited the car. Raised his hood against the downpour. Took in his surroundings with his hands in his pockets and furtive glances in every direction. It was just him, the heavy sky, and the pouring rain. No one waited for him in wet shadows or watched from dripping hedgerows.

The metal fence was rusted and sagging, patched with dead leaves, litter and scraps of paper. Weeds had emerged through cracks in the crumbling asphalt. He shook the padlocked gates then paced the perimeter until he found a hole in the fence, probably made by local children or someone who'd reckoned there would be valuables to steal inside the park. The hole was just big enough for him. He pulled back jutting metal barbs and crawled through the opening, dirtying his hands and knees.

He stood on the other side and wiped his palms on his coat. The park opened before him in all its grand filth and squalor. A miserable stain in a sweet, corrupted world. He wondered if anyone had mourned for this place.

Rows of dilapidated caravans had been left to fall into ruin. He walked among them, peering through clouded windows dirty with grime and grease. And he watched the windows for signs of movement and imagined white leering faces pressed against the glass to observe him as he walked past. The park was silent, not a place to loiter without ill intent or steady nerves. The hairs on his arms stiffened with the feeling that the caravans were still occupied and the residents were hiding from him, as though they were not fit to be looked upon. Things to be shunned, all fungal and banished to rotting rooms.

He spat by his feet, cast his eyes around.

Nature was reclaiming this place; weeds and wild copses of overgrown grass, blossoms of fungi and black toadstools prospering beneath caravans. Walls mottled with mould and lichen and sagging with damp. A sign hanging from one rusted chain, bleached and worn.

The rain did not stop.

In an open grassed area a burnt-out car skulked, dripping water from its scalded angles of metal and gutted insides. Melted tyres like nonsense shapes hardened into obsidian. The grass around the car was blackened and scorched and smelled of petrol. Part of Ben was disappointed not to see bones among the charred ruin.

He called out for Doyle as he moved among the sodden walkways, kicking at empty food tins and soft drinks cans.

No one answered. The silence followed him down the walkways and between the slumped shapes where the windows were once filled with light and the sounds of televisions, radios and arguing couples were all that could be heard.

The sky churned black and enraged like a manic titan in its death throes. Hammers of the gods.

Ben arrived at a large, twisted elm tree growing at the centre of the park. Thin dark branches reached towards the sky. Wizened and scarred. He was an inferior creature in the tree's presence, hunched against the rain and shivering from the cold. His teeth chattered. He quickly dispelled the notion that the tree was dormant, hibernating through the lean months of winter, ready to awaken now that flesh had arrived. He imagined a tree with roots that took nourishment from the buried bodies of those it strangled and crushed with its busy limbs.

Photos of children hung on frayed string from the branches, black and white, sepia and colour, most of them faded with age. Different decades and fashions. None of the boys and girls appeared any older than twelve, and some of them smiled, but most of them just stared blankly, nothing in their faces but a dour acceptance as they looked into the distance. The bleached white of their eyes must have been due to the condition of the photos. Girls with blonde hair in curls and pigtails. Young boys with cowlicks and freckles. They wore odd socks and mittens, scuffed trainers and buckled shoes. The ragged clothing of orphans and unwanted children.

There had to be over fifty photos stirring and flapping in the wind. Ben looked away, and his eyes scanned the horizon through a gap between the caravans, where rain swept over funnels of black. He called out for Doyle, again, but his voice went unanswered.

He wrapped his arms around himself and sheltered under the elm. The rain roared and the clouds moved like rushing water. The ground beneath the shaking bough was rippled with bulging roots.

A fork of lightning in the east. Distant thunder followed. He had to move from under the tree before the lightning found him.

A shape appeared in his peripheral vision. He turned. Doyle had appeared out of the rain, a silent hooded figure.

Ben curled his fingers around the knife in his pocket and shifted his feet. The ground squirmed underneath his shoes.

Doyle nodded. Pallid, drawn face under his hood. His eyes were large and strained. His mouth twitched.

"Follow me," Doyle said.

~

Ben walked behind Doyle, but kept his distance and his hand clenched around the knife. He blinked away spitting rain and wiped it from his face. More thunder in the distance, like continents splitting and shifting.

Doyle led him to a caravan that looked much the same as the other neglected dwellings, drooping and bowed, with cracked walls and growths of moss. There was light in the window. Doyle opened the door and they went inside. Ben could hear his own heartbeat. The caravan stank of old damp. The roof was leaking, water trickling down one wall onto faded linoleum. Mildew and mouse shit. The floor sucked at Ben's shoes as he stepped into the light from a Coleman lantern that revealed a kitchenette and cupboards without doors; a living space at one end of the caravan and a dining table set within a seated area. Worktops covered in dust, desiccated insects, and rodent spoor.

There was something on the dining table, wrapped in a bin bag. A crumpled shape covered in black plastic.

Doyle closed the door. The yellow light put marsh-glow in the man's eyes.

"What's going on?" Ben said. "Why did you call me out here in the pissing rain?"

"I'm sorry for calling you out of the blue, but this is important. You're part of this, Ben. We're all part of this."

"What are you talking about?"

Doyle held up his hands. "Let me show you." He walked to the dining table and Ben reluctantly followed. He left enough distance between himself and the table for him to produce the knife and use it before whatever was in the bag emerged and came at him.

"You won't believe what I've found," Doyle said.

"Tell me."

Doyle gently tipped the bag, and a loose gathering of pale wet flesh spilled onto the table.

Ben wasn't sure what he was looking at, but then his eyes adjusted to the thing splayed before him, and he took a step back. His mouth opened and his tongue waggled, but he couldn't speak.

It was boneless and glistening with sprawling white tendrils that flopped over the side of the table and touched the floor, beneath a fleshy bell the size of a dustbin lid. Wet muscle, skin and meat. Epidermal folds all slick and gelatinous. It was approximately four feet in length and two feet wide. Ben glimpsed a moist red maw under the bell. Fluid dripped to the floor from its unravelled body. Something that lived in the darkness of ocean depths.

It smelled like brine and dead fish. An eye-watering stink. Ben covered his nose with one hand.

There was a *wrongness* about it.

Ben's heart was full and trembling. He glanced at Doyle. "You found a jellyfish?"

Doyle wiped his mouth as a half-smile creased the lower portion of his face under the thick beard. There was a faint tremor to his hand. "I found it earlier when I was walking in the fields."

"It's something you'd find washed up on a beach," Ben said.

"Then what was it doing so far inland?"

"I've heard of fish being picked up by typhoons

and hurricanes and carried miles inland. Maybe that's what happened here..."

"We haven't had anything like that," said Doyle. "This is England. And it's too big to be picked up by a strong wind."

Ben felt stupid for suggesting it. "I don't know. Maybe someone found it by the sea and brought it back here. I'm not sure why they would do that, though."

The men looked at each other.

"I saw it in a dream," Doyle said. "I saw where it came from."

"What? Don't be ridiculous," Ben said. A cold, thick sweat broke out between his shoulder blades.

"I saw it," said Doyle.

Ben stepped back. "I don't believe you."

"It's true. I saw it in a dream and then I found it in the fields."

Ben sighed. "This is preposterous. I should never have come out here." But he looked at the thing on the table and found that he couldn't turn away.

Doyle stared at the dead creature, awestruck and pallid, a shaking tension in his arms. His beard dripped water. His lips parted and a glistening string of saliva hung between them.

The rain fell, kicked and pulled by the wind. The caravan swayed. The lantern shook on its stand and turned the men into peeled shadows upon the wall.

"The dreams," said Doyle. "You have to know about the dreams."

~

Ben drove to Doyle's house. His head was a tumult of thoughts and clouds as black as those that filled the sky. His hands shook on the steering wheel. Doyle sat next to him with the invertebrate wrapped in the bin bag on his lap. He kept coughing, intermittently, into one hand, and it sounded like the gasp of something rising from filthy water to take its first breath.

Doyle's dog greeted them at the door, sniffing the air that came with them and the smells on their clothes. Its eyes turned towards the bag in Doyle's arms and it backed away, unsure of the stink coming from within. Ben sympathised. The hound started growling, baring its teeth, eyes bulging with fear. Its muscled legs tensed and shook.

Doyle shouted at the dog to be quiet, and the wolfhound fled to its bed in the corner. Doyle took the dead thing to a back room. On the way there Ben made sure not to look at the paintings on the walls.

~

The jellyfish was laid on a large wooden table, exposed to the four walls and the bare light bulb humming directly above it, throwing shadows that seemed to twitch when Ben glimpsed them in his peripheral vision. He stood against the far wall, keeping his distance from the dead creature, worried that it might eventually tremble into some terrible parody of life and attack those who had awoken it. He lit a cigarette and sucked on it until the fog in his head cleared.

Doyle poured vodka out of an old bottle. He handed one tumbler to Ben and they downed the shots. Ben grimaced and coughed. The burn of harsh chemicals in his chest. His eyes watered.

"I get it from an old friend of mine in Poland," Doyle said. "Tastes like fertiliser, but it does the job."

"It's disgusting," Ben said.

"Another one?"

"Yes, please."

Doyle poured again.

Ben sipped the vodka and looked around the room until his eyes fell upon the dead thing. "Did you really see it in your dreams?"

Doyle stood by the table, looking down at the creature. "I did." There was a tremor in his mouth. "There have been visitations. Emergences. Incursions."

"What do you mean?"

Air escaped Doyle's mouth. "Holes in the world."

"I don't understand."

"It has something to do with the dreams," Doyle said.

Ben tipped the rest of his drink down his throat, said nothing.

"You look tired, Ben."

"Haven't been sleeping too well."

"You've had the dreams, haven't you?"

Ben chewed on a fingernail and looked at his feet with the urge to walk out of there and drive away. Never come back. Leave Doyle and this madness behind.

"Look at me," Doyle said.

Ben looked at him.

Doyle nodded at the slack thing on the table. "This has something to do with the dreams. I suspect that the whole village is having them. I think it's connected to when you collapsed in the fields. I've had the dreams for years, but they've gotten worse recently."

"They're just dreams," Ben said, even though his heart raced and his face flushed with heat. Acid frothed in the pit of his stomach. "And that thing on the table could be from anywhere. Someone might have dumped it in the fields for a joke, for all we know."

"It's getting worse."

"I should leave."

"Stay. You need to know what's happening."

"I'm sorry, Doyle. I don't need this; I've got my own problems."

"Please don't go."

Ben's phone chirped. He pulled it from his pocket and checked the text message. It was from his father.

Please come home, lad.

Seven

Johnny Cash sang about darkness.

Ben guided the car along the wet roads through the village. He drove slowly, mindful of the cramped streets and cars parked at awkward angles beside the pavements. The windscreen wipers shrieked and scraped over glass. The heaters melted condensation from the windows.

He flicked the headlights on and slowed the car to negotiate a tight corner. A man was standing in the rain, by the roadside, facing the stone wall of an old building. His back was turned to Ben, and he wore a bright yellow waterproof coat with a pointed hood that gave the impression of a long neck and head. He was wiping his face hurriedly. Before Ben turned away he was sure the man had spat blood onto the pavement.

Further down the street, a front door was open and a woman dwelled on the threshold. She raised her face and regarded him with a pudgy, bovine-like expression, then retreated into the house and shut the door.

When he reached Dad's house the rain lessened to drizzle and gradually stopped. Ben walked inside and found his father in the living room, hunched in his armchair, his eyes wet and glassy. He glanced at Ben, raised his pallid face, and wiped his eyes.

"Dad, what's wrong?" Ben stood by the armchair, unsure whether to place his hand on his father's shoulder.

Dad swallowed, closed his eyes so tight and forcefully that his face almost collapsed. He leaned forward and covered his mouth with one hand. When he looked at Ben again, the skin of his face trembled as though tiny worms moved underneath. His eyes were red and sore and tired.

"I had a dream," Dad said, whiskey fumes on his breath.

The mention of dreams made Ben's stomach lurch.

Dad was shaking his head as he stared at the old stains on his trousers. He poured a large glass of whiskey and downed it in three hurried gulps. He gasped then wiped his mouth. Blood flushed in his face.

"What do you mean?" Ben said.

His father nodded at the patio doors where grey winter light encroached. He looked outside and his eyes widened, wet enough to slip and tumble from his face.

He put his hand on his father's shoulder. "Dad..."

Ben's father swivelled his head towards him, as if awakened from a silent fugue. He wiped his eyes again and placed his spectacles over them, and his pupils appeared large and black like marble. Shadows under his eyes. The remaining strands of hair on his head were greasy and unkempt.

"Something was watching us. Watching me. Watching all of us. I could touch it, but it was made of nothing, and its shadow fell over me and I drowned within it. Then I woke up, and it was still raining, and something came out of the rain and stood at the patio doors, looking in at me. It was your mother. But it wasn't your mother. It came to give us a message. It was a messenger. A herald.

Ben's mouth went dry and something itched behind his eyes. "What was the message?"

"One word," Dad said. "Communion."

~

Later, after the grey light turned to black, Ben went into the back garden to smoke a cigarette and watch the shivering constellations emerge through the veil of night sky.

The temperature had dropped to near freezing, turning the rain-soaked ground to hard earth and frost. Faint glimmer of the moon. Puddles were becoming ice and by the morning they would be stains of glittering silver and mud-brown.

Ben's thoughts were muddled and disordered. Chaotic. Splintered into screaming fragments. He exhaled smoke from his lungs and thought about the jellyfish-thing, its acrid stink and the limp wetness of its tendrils.

He took a final, long drag and bowed his head.

Ben dropped the cigarette and smothered it with the heel of his shoe. He put his hands in his pockets for warmth. The night was quiet beyond the garden. The scrubland past the fence whispered of earthworms burrowing and nocturnal hunts through broken thickets of weeds. He raised his face to the sky and saw that the stars were different than they were seconds ago. Out of place and order. Unknown constellations flared and dwindled. The revolutions of cold, dead galaxies.

The stars weren't right.

~

They ate breakfast at the dining table. Ben chewed on buttered toast and sipped strong coffee. His father sat across from him, hunched and tatty, a frayed shape of limbs and skin in an unravelling dressing gown.

"I drank too much," Dad said, picking something from his eye. "I must have dreamt of seeing your mother outside. That was all."

"You should take it easy today, Dad," said Ben.

"I think I'll go back to bed in a bit. I'm tired. My head hurts."

Ben tore a piece of toast into two halves and stared at the table.

~

The frost lingered on the ground. There was no wind today and the sky was low and white. The weather forecast predicted snow in the coming days. Ben wore a thick jumper inside the house and warmed the living room with an electric heater that smelled like burnt hair when it overheated. Dad retired to bed and plummeted through the depths of daytime television with a pot of sweet tea and a tin of biscuits.

Ben watched the day through misted windows. The only sounds in the house were the creaking of Dad's bed as he shuffled and fidgeted, mixed with the hollow chatter of a game show he was watching. Ben watched the taps drip and the clocks tick. He chucked medication down his throat and chased it with cold coffee. He stared blankly at a watercolour painting of an English lake in summer, trying to remember what the sun's heat felt like on his face. But all he could recall was the cold.

He watched snow clouds unfurl and descend. He tried to distract himself from the fears coiling inside the wet chambers of his mind. Thoughts of jellyfish with stinging tendrils and suffocating membranes turned his guts to slop.

Just after midday he looked out over the back garden from an upstairs window. There were people stood on the scrubland beyond the garden. He counted eight: four men, four women. They were inanimate figures swaddled in thin layers of clothing, staring at the ground by their feet. Then some of them began swaying, and the movement of their shoulders was vaguely hypnotic, almost graceful, as though they were listening to the whispered songs of the universe, a hive mind sharing special secrets.

Ben watched them, stood back from the window in case they noticed him. He didn't want to see their faces; he shouldn't have to see their faces. Intuition told him it wasn't a good idea.

The occasional gust of cold wind stirred their hair. Eventually, they dispersed in different directions and Ben watched them leave, unsettled by the methodical movements of their bodies.

Beyond the scrubland, a woman was standing in her back garden, facing Ben. A nightdress barely restrained the pale, lumpy folds of her body. She raised a hand to him in greeting. He returned the gesture then retreated slowly from the window until he was out of her sight.

~

Ben felt lethargic and drained; a bird with broken

wings. He sloped around the house, losing time and memories. A pulsing, dull pain in his head. Mouth scraped of moisture, his tongue slow over his teeth. It felt like he was caught in a fever-dream, but the dream was outside, and the spaces he filled were pockets of reality that were shrinking. The thought of opening a door and stepping outside into the cold air made his chest heavy and tight. Creeping dread. Reluctantly, he opened a window to breathe in some clean air. Cabin fever made his skin itch. He thought he heard a police siren in the distance. He watched repeats of old monster films. Bad actors chased by Harryhausen creations. He applauded when Sinbad killed the sabre-toothed cat at the end of *Sinbad and the Eye of the Tiger*.

After watching the old films he flicked through a hive of channels full of faces and skin. Reality shows, gardening programmes and repeats of game shows where hosts in tailored suits preened and minced, and contestants with mullets and charity-shop fashions cheered and chattered towards the camera.

The television flickered; the picture blurred then cleared, then blurred again. Jagged lines appeared and turned the face of the game show host into a Boschian travesty. Then static and snow filled the screen, and out of the muddled sounds pouring from the speakers a desolate howling resonated. It was a sound from lost depths and black canyons.

Cold sweat broke out on his face and he pawed for the remote control. When the television fell silent and dark, he shivered among the stained cushions, flustered and pale. A whisper inside his head voiced unpleasant suggestions. He splashed water on his face from the kitchen sink and looked out at the street cast in grey light. He thought he'd glimpsed a tall figure move away from his car and down the road. No one else was out there.

He worried about what would happen to him if he went outside, left the boundaries of the house, the garden, and walked out into the street. He was struck with the irrational fear that he would be seized and dragged away, or something would descend from the low clouds and pluck him from the ground as if he were a small, scurrying mammal.

You are a small mammal, in the grand scheme of things.

Ben moved around the house, running fingers over flagging wallpaper and examining minute fractures in the walls. He pored through Dad's history books and some old photos of Dad's short career playing for the village football team before a buckled knee had forced him to retire.

At the kitchen sink, he scrubbed his blemished skin with his fingers. He looked around the kitchen with clear eyes and recalled his earliest memory of looking up at his mother as she washed dishes and smiled down at him where he stood now. He must have been around three or four, then, back when *Mr. Men* and tinned spaghetti were the most important things in his life.

He put out a lit match on his forearm to prove he was real. A rush of blood answered the sharp second of pain. Was pain the height of being alive? Was life a lucid dream of meat and pumping hearts?

Ben returned to the sofa with a tumbler of Dad's whiskey and the previous day's newspaper.

~

A dream. Or something similar to a dream.

They don't live in the water...

A world between worlds. A swarming darkness of death-sounds and bestial cries. The void expelled inhuman echoes. Monsters dwelling in abyssal ravines, and they could see the hopes and failures of dreaming apes. The jellyfish drifted through the darkness, bioluminescent and silent, a flock of thousands. Whip-like tentacles hanging from umbrella-shaped bells, gelatinous and pulsing. The glow of their marble bodies lit his face, stung his eyes and filled his mouth with ghost-light. He stood among them unharmed, and their grace broke his heart because they were just things to be preyed upon by predators beyond the comprehension of human minds.

Something watched him.

The jellyfish flock shattered in all directions, evading a hunter. He was reminded of a whale scooping plankton into its mouth. Gaping darkness opened before Ben. Something else was there, and its power sent his heart into convulsions.

Black star, black sun.

He screamed, but it was lost below the sound of wailing mouths.

Ben was consumed by the swelling darkness and it opened the soft parts of him, burrowing into his mind, absorbing his memories and fear and desperation, welcoming him to a life without pain and grief.

He was given communion.

Eight

Ben awoke whimpering and crying. His nose was bleeding and tremors wracked his limbs. He stemmed the flow of blood with a tissue and downed what remained of the whiskey by his side.

He rushed to the bathroom and vomited a weak, black gruel that tasted like burnt treacle into the toilet. He sat on the floor and leaned against the toilet bowl, gasping as he wiped tears from his eyes.

After he dried his mouth and caught his breath, he went to the mirror above the sink and examined his face. He looked like something recently exhumed, and he spat into the sink and stared into his sore, pink-rimmed eyes. There was a bruise under his jaw. He held onto the sink, too scared to let go.

"Black star," he whispered.

~

His father was slipping into sleep when Ben entered the bedroom. The bedside lamp washed the room in soft light. The television was muted while an old war film played.

"Dad."

His father woke with a stifled yelp, eyes wide and wet.

"Ben," he said, and his voice was slurred and low. "I don't want to fall asleep..."

Ben sat on the edge of the bed by Dad's legs. The mattress sunk and creaked beneath him.

"I've had the dreams," said Ben.

His father looked at his hands laid upon his lap, and they were crinkled and worn, textured like rough wood. He looked up at Ben. His face had aged badly, haggard and dry, harmed by the passage of years. Atrophy and decline undermining his body. His eyes were bloodshot and moist. Ben was shocked at the frail, wizened frame of his father mired in the old bed.

"The dreams are getting worse," his father said, as confirmation.

"What have you seen in them?" Ben asked.

Dad swallowed. His shoulders sagged and he looked like a thing made of brittle wood stuffed into faded garments. "I saw darkness. Somewhere beyond here. I felt something watching me, getting closer. I didn't see it, but it snatched me into the dark, and I was absorbed. Then I was in the fields outside the village, and the ground was covered with the rotting bodies of jellyfish, all stinking and twitching. Then I woke up."

"Christ," said Ben. He scratched at his face as he thought of slopping wet limbs.

"I don't know what's happening," Dad said. "I

keep thinking I hear things – animal sounds and shrill barks. Sometimes I can feel the ground grinding, and shifting."

"I dreamt that I was in the darkness," said Ben. "A place between worlds. Sounds ridiculous, I know. I saw the jellyfish and they were beautiful. Then the *other* arrived and it took me too, made me a part of it. The black star."

"Communion," Dad whispered, with reverence and dread.

Ben looked at him, said nothing. His jaw was frozen and stiff. The muscles in his face ached.

The television flickered, then died, and left them in silence.

~

Ben's phone rang. Doyle. He ignored it and sipped his mug of tea. Two minutes later Doyle called again. Ben didn't move.

A shrill chirp. A voicemail message. Reluctantly, he put the phone to his ear and listened.

"Ben; it's Doyle. I need to talk to you. It's getting worse. The dreams are changing people. It could be the end of all things. I finally saw it – I finally saw the black star."

Nine

Ben had run out of cigarettes. The craving for nicotine was an itch inside his skull, inflaming the soft tissue of his brain. He couldn't dull the need, especially after what Dad had told him, along with Doyle's voicemail. He daydreamed of writhing smoke and ash and tar gliding through his lungs. It was delicious.

He hadn't returned Doyle's call; he was too scared to hear what other secrets the man had to reveal.

The end of all things.

Ben couldn't stand it any longer. Shrugging on his coat, he crept from the house while his father slept. He made sure to lock the front door.

He stepped out into the silent world.

~

Ben parked his car outside the shop. The street was empty, but he felt the heat of careful observation from windows above and around him. He looked towards the school across the road, where the playground was deserted, windblown and grey. No chattering children or the scrape and slap of small feet. A silence filled the small spaces and dim places. He looked up and down the street, folding his arms to his chest and shifting his feet upon the dimpled tarmac. He thought there was a noise overhead, and he looked up at the ceiling of pale cloud, telling himself he hadn't seen the rippling of something long and worm-like move above the village.

The door alert chimed as he entered the shop. He wiped his feet on the mat and stepped into narrow aisles lined with stacks of canned goods and dusty shelves, where the air smelled of furniture polish and vinegar. Paper sacks of potatoes were piled in a corner, dusted with a fine layer of dirt and grit. Pineapple chunks in syrup and tins of dog food with scratched labels. Condensed milk and jars of marmalade and jam sat alongside Roy Orbison CDs. A refrigerated section of milk, cheese, and a pot of yoghurt past its best day. Metal trays of root vegetables that resembled deformed appendages had been squeezed between shelves of waxen and overripe fruit. The floor was the colour of cream on the turn. The walls sighed as Ben moved slowly among the aisles, and he stopped to search through a spinning rack of old paperback novels. The books were faded and creased, tattered spines and pages yellowed at their edges. The rack creaked as he turned it and glanced over books with front covers of screaming mouths, severed body parts, and knives dripping blood, all written by pulp writers long forgotten. They had weird titles. One was called *Maniac Gods*.

Ben picked up a newspaper, a box of Jaffa Cakes, a pack of soft toilet roll and two cans of Red Bull, placing them into the metal wire basket slung over his arm. When he was finished searching the aisles he placed the basket on the counter and smiled politely at the old woman behind it. She smiled back at him, and he recognised her as the woman who'd grinned at him in the church the previous Sunday.

"It's quiet today," Ben said, and cleared his throat. The counter was flanked by displays of chewing gum, chocolate bars and toffees to tempt the sweet-toothed. There was a scrunched-up tissue on the woman's side of the counter, and her hand hovered near it then retreated to her stomach, where she held both hands together, prayer-like and serene. Ben noticed a reddened scratch mark at her left temple that looked recent and stood out against the pallor of her face like a birthmark. Her hair was scraped back from her forehead, severe and slickened above a grey cardigan that hung over her meatless form like an oversized shawl.

Her lips were red and wet. Her smile was painted on, below glazed eyes with little light within them. And her grin faltered at the edges of her mouth.

"Yes, that's right. Quiet. Anything else you need?"

"Uh, oh yes." Ben fiddled with his wallet and plucked a twenty pound note from the dry folds. "A pack of twenty Lambert and Butler, please."

She turned to the cigarette display behind her, moving like she was manipulated by an unseen puppeteer beneath the counter. She wiped her mouth. Ben noticed there was a red lesion on the nape of her thin neck.

The silence, punctuated by each breath she took through her painted mouth, unsettled Ben. He coughed, glancing out the window at the empty street.

"I really should give up," he said. "Isn't good for me."

"It doesn't matter," the woman said, with her back to him.

"Excuse me?"

She turned and faced him. "I seem to have run out of them. But I'm sure there're some in stock out the back. I'll return in a moment." Her red smile gleamed, and she vanished through the doorway behind the counter, sharp-heeled shoes clicking on the floor.

Ben waited, tapping one foot on the grime-dusted tiling. He looked down at the floor and wondered when the tiling had been installed and why it had been left to deteriorate to such a state.

The clock ticked and clicked like a mechanical insect studying him from the wall. The back of his neck tingled coldly, and he had to resist turning around to regard the aisles behind him and the hands he imagined to be reaching for his shoulders. No one had entered the shop since he'd been there, and there were no thin, sighing figures watching him from the back of the shop.

Minutes passed. He was keen to return to his father's house and shelter behind its walls. The empty streets unnerved him, loosened his insides. A figure moved past the window, and Ben caught it just in time to see the flash of a yellow coat followed by a barked voice, like a warning or a threat.

He looked towards the doorway, expecting the woman to reappear. How long did it take to find some cigarettes? He called out, offered his assistance, but it wasn't until he was about to leave the shop that he was answered by a voice that became a low mewl through stifled lips. A sound more animal than human. And then the voice whispered his name. Maybe it was a call for help.

Ben swallowed hard and breathed quickly through his mouth, hesitating with his hands dawdling at his sides. His eyes didn't leave the darkened doorway into which the woman had vanished.

He checked his watch; he couldn't leave his father alone for too long, but he had to see if the woman was okay.

"Shit," he muttered, and clenched his jaw.

Reluctantly, with his heart flinching, he moved

slowly behind the counter, whispering an old poem to himself as he stepped through the doorway into a place of darkness and silence.

~

He started down the swollen-walled corridor, and as he neared the door at the far end, light spilling underneath it, the sound of heavy sobbing grew louder until there was no doubt the woman was inside. To the left of the door was a throat of darkened stairs and a small bathroom painted in dour shades.

He pushed the door open and froze when he found her crying on her knees upon the stone floor of the storeroom. A light bulb washed tall shelves and cardboard boxes in stark yellow. The room was windowless and shadows breathed at the pulsing corners of the walls. Ben could smell old plaster and faded paint.

The woman was perpendicular to Ben, her head bowed, frail shoulders hitching as she pawed at the floor with veined and fumbling hands that made a terrible scratching with their nails. Her shadow loomed away from her and seemed too gangly and fidgety. He imagined her with more limbs than she actually had. Ben shivered. When she turned towards him, he stepped back against the doorframe. Her face was slack and wet. Tears glistened in her glass eyes. Her mouth was open and sagging, and her teeth were smeared with blood. She opened her jaws wider, drawing in stale breath and the dank smell of the walls, and let out a mournful wail like something last heard across the mists of prehistoric marshes. She held one hand out to him, her fingers moving like spiders' legs. A dry wheeze from between her stained teeth. The blood must have been her own because there was nothing else there she could have fastened her mouth upon.

He went to her and lifted her, gently, onto wilting legs. The stink of her was overwhelming, like the reek of a wretched foal pulled from a mother horse. She rested her head against his chest, hot and weightless, and sagged against him, a skeleton in papyrus skin under her dampened clothes. Her hands, like talons, found purchase upon him and were surprisingly insistent at his coat until he guided them away. When he looked down at her tear-streaked, pallid face, there was no hope in her eyes and the red stain of her mouth was obscene.

"Help me," she said, gasping. "Please help me. I've been having such bad dreams lately."

She let out a distressed cry that pierced Ben's chest, and sobbed into her hands, fragile and dismal. She muttered something incomprehensible through the froth on her lips, a low scrape of vocal chords and wet tongue. It sounded low and unpleasant, like a whispered curse. Unintelligible words and broken sentences. Her red mouth was running.

"It's okay," Ben said. "Let's sit you down somewhere and I'll get some help." He turned and steered her towards a wooden stool by the nearest wall, but was halted by the tall dark shape of Reverend Glass in the doorway.

The woman let out a slow, dragging breath.

"Is there a problem?" Glass said. He appeared concerned, face tight and drawn, defined by dark lines. Then his features relaxed and he wiped his mouth with the back of his sleeve.

"She's ill," Ben said. "I found her on the floor. I think it was some sort of seizure."

The reverend entered the room, trailing his shadow. The woman shivered, flinched. She looked up at Glass.

"I'll take it from here," Glass said. "Thank you, Ben. Thanks for your help."

"She's sick," Ben said.

"Undoubtedly," said Glass, "but it's nothing I can't handle. Sally here is prone to bouts of confusion. She hasn't been herself for a while. In and out of the hospital, you see. All sorts of tests and scans. Grim stuff. She's old, Ben."

Glass gently took the woman from Ben's hands and whispered something in her ear. She nodded faintly. Then Glass looked at Ben. The light made his face severe and sharp.

"Dementia. Poor old girl. It's getting worse and worse."

"Why was she left in charge of the shop, then?"

Glass frowned. "The girl that usually helps out called in sick today. I was supposed to pop over and give Sylvia a hand, hence why I'm here."

"Shouldn't we call an ambulance?"

Glass shook his head too soon, too quick. "No. I'll take care of her. I'll call Sally's daughter in the next village. No need for you to stay, Ben."

"Are you sure?"

"Absolutely. It's better if you leave. Sally doesn't know you and if she sees you hanging around the place when she becomes lucid again, she'll have a fright. She's very wary of strangers."

"Okay," Ben muttered. "I guess I am a stranger here." The light bulb flickered. The air he breathed felt dirty and tainted.

Glass enfolded the woman's slight form, and she sobbed silently, her hands at her face, his spindly arms around her shoulders. He guided her from the storeroom with hands that were too white and smooth.

Ben watched them climb the stairs. He went back out to the store, gathered his shopping, and left the money on the counter. He didn't take the change he was owed.

Ten

On the way to the car, he passed a house with its front door wide open. Someone was laughing beyond the doorway. Harsh, cruel laughter, like a taunt or an insult. Breathless. He kept walking. He reached his car and fumbled with the key, and when he opened the door it knocked against his knee, because he had turned to meet the sound of slapping feet behind him. But there was nothing there. He climbed into his seat and locked himself behind metal and glass. A muffled voice called out from somewhere behind the car. His hand was shaking as he tried to find the ignition slot, and his heart rose into his gullet, swollen and hot. Finally, the key found its place, and he turned it towards the engine. He kept glancing up beyond the bonnet, worried there were people approaching the car, creeping up to it so they could open the doors and climb inside. He exhaled with relief when it started on the first attempt, and looked out at the street.

Nothing moved out there.

He drove back through the village, and he told himself that the distorted, writhing shapes glimpsed in the side mirrors were merely parts of his imagination, nothing more than shadow and anxiety. His head pulsed and buzzed. Acid broiled in his stomach. He had to keep blinking sweat from his eyes, and couldn't stop thinking about the old woman and the look on Reverend Glass's face as he guided her up the stairs.

Ben reached his father's house and parked out front. As he climbed out he noticed a woman staring down at him from an upstairs window in the house across the street. Her chalk-white, doughy and expressionless face was framed by strands of lank hair that seemed too slick and oily upon her thin shoulders. Her hooded eyes were the same colour as the shadows behind her stilted form. She was heavily pregnant, her pale hands resting upon her swollen stomach.

Ben raised one hand to her.

She stared at him and did not respond.

He turned away and hurried to the house, shaking the cold from his limbs as he glanced back over his shoulder.

Once he was inside, he made sure to lock the doors.

~

Ben closed the curtains to the downstairs windows. The wind rattled the walls and whistled down the chimney into the dark, cold fireplace, where it stirred tiny plumes of soot into the air. He sat on the sofa, nursing a cigarette between his fingers and dabbing its ash into the old clay bowl. He thought about dreams and nightmares, and wondered how much longer he could stay awake before his body began to shut down from exhaustion.

He downed the cans of Red Bull and gritted his teeth against the acid reflux in his chest. He drank black coffee that burned his lips and tongue. He slapped his face to keep the blood quick under his skin.

Dad was asleep upstairs. Ben hoped that if he was dreaming he wouldn't remember when he woke up.

He finished the cigarette and took another from the packet, lighting it with fingers not entirely steady. From his wallet he pulled the photo of him and Emily on top of Trench Hill, just after he had proposed to her under the large oak tree upon its summit. They had been returning from visiting his parents one Sunday evening during a distant summer, and Ben had suggested stopping to walk up the hill and appreciate the views of the surrounding fields as the sun fell. Once they were under the tree, Ben had dropped to one knee, his heart tumbling and rising, and asked her the question he'd been holding back for weeks.

Emily's smile had told him her answer.

Ben returned the photo to his wallet and put it out of sight.

He drew heavily on the cigarette and tried not to imagine silent hands pawing at the windows from outside. Smoke slipped from the holes in his face and rose to the ceiling. His mouth tasted of bile and bad meat, his eyes ached and he wanted to sleep. He wanted so badly to sleep.

The house sighed. Outside, the wind picked up and pushed at the tired walls, and the village was silent.

~

He had dreamed of symbols carved into his skin with a blade of bone sharpened to a fine needlepoint. Twisted shapes and patterns he didn't recognise made him feel nauseated and confused when he remembered them.

In the stinging light of the bedside lamp he checked his stomach to make sure it wasn't spoiled and gouged by his own hand, and was relieved to see his skin intact and free of mutilation. He had awoken in his bed with a thundering heart and a gasp stuck in his throat. After he'd collected his thoughts he sat on the edge of the bed and held his head in his hands until the nausea in his chest faded.

He couldn't remember going to bed. He was fully clothed Time was missing. His last memory was of smoking on the sofa while listening to the walls creak and sigh.

Checking his phone he saw it was almost eleven o'clock. The thought of those dark streets, roads and lanes outside the house made his heart dwindle and his legs weaken. He padded to the door. The landing light was on when he emerged from his room, and the house was silent. Something cold clenched his heart when he saw that Dad's bedroom door was open.

~

Ben stepped into the room. The bed was empty save for tangled sheets and a scattering of biscuit crumbs on the mattress. Empty beer cans and a dinner plate of leftovers filled the bedside table. Dirty cutlery discarded on the floor. The faint smell of sweat and body musk.

"Dad?"

He dropped to his knees, wincing, and checked under the bed. But his father wasn't there. He remembered how he had found Dad last week, standing in the front doorway, transfixed by the dark and whoever was calling to him out into the cold.

Ben stumbled downstairs. He checked the living room and looked out into the back garden, but it was deserted.

He stepped into the kitchen and halted, breathing hard through his nose. The front door was open, and the cold air that pushed into the house ran across his skin and made his teeth chatter. Frost was at the windows. Light from the kitchen spilled onto the front garden, painting a ghost upon the lawn. The house across the road was a hulking shadow without illumination or warmth in its windows.

His father was out there, beyond him, beyond the light.

Eleven

Ben shrugged on a coat and laced trainers over his bare feet. He grabbed the torch from under the kitchen sink and with one unsure hand slipped a carving knife into his coat pocket.

With his phone and keys stuffed into his jeans, he went outside, where the air was like ice against his face and moon-shadows spread tall and long. He searched the front garden, and the back garden again, afraid that the shifting torchlight would reveal his father's frozen face, glassy and white among the grass and sickly shrubs.

He found nothing, and the faint relief dwindled against the rising panic in his chest. Tiny feet scurried in the neighbouring garden, night creatures fleeing from his clumsy footfalls. He locked the house and went out onto the scrubland beyond the back garden. The moon was full and silver, a polished coin tarnished by scars.

It was a small comfort to recognise the constellations tonight.

~

He traipsed over rents and divots, molehills and burrows, sweeping the ground with the torch beam.

Small mounds of dog shit. The dirt reeked of badger and fox urine. A plastic bag stirred and rustled out of the night like a lost ghost, pulling a frightened gasp from his mouth. The houses beyond the scrubland were dark and silent, full of dreamers in soft beds and wrapped blankets. The night breeze stirred the knotted clumps of yellowed grass around his feet, and he turned each way, scanning with the torch because he could hear voices among this lonely place. He covered the ground in hesitant strides, eyes flicking right and left, then into the middle distance where the scrubland continued ahead. He rubbed his eyes when he glimpsed a loping shadow twenty feet to his right that melted into the fringes of the field. When he shone his torch towards it there was nothing.

"Dad!" His voice echoed pitifully in the dark.

After searching the scrubland, Ben moved onto the streets. The sodium glare of the streetlights formed too many shadows, and they were twisted, fluttering things joined to him. No one was out this late. Not at this hour. The village went to sleep early, especially when the lull of winter was upon the streets.

He remembered from his late teens and early twenties, stumbling back through the village after a night out in one of the nearby towns, usually when he and his mates couldn't afford the whole taxi fare home and had to be dropped outside the village because they'd spent all their money on cheap lager and shots, kebabs, and drinks for young women in little skirts. A few times he had to walk home alone after losing his mates in a nightclub. And he had experienced a sense of awe and euphoria because he was the only soul on the streets and they belonged to him.

There were no awestruck feelings now. The streets were cold and euphoria had died with his youth. He searched the churchyard and stepped among the graves of the long-dead and ruined. No more dreams for them. He checked his mother's grave, hoping to find Dad there, but when he stood by the graveside he was the only mourner in the dark. There was no sign of his father at his grandparents' graves either.

Shivering, he rubbed his arms to coax some warmth into his blood. The cold made his eyes ache and his jaw flinch. Awful visions of Dad made a home in his thoughts; that he or some unsuspecting visitor would find his father the next morning, stiff and frozen, curled foetal against the cold which had killed him.

Ben walked the streets as the hours slipped away, searching through gardens, open yards, driveways, and small lanes that were no wider than his shoulders. There was no trace of his father, so he returned to the house, hoping to find Dad either passed out on the sofa or slumped in the kitchen with a cup of coffee and ready apology.

The empty house sighed around him. Ben called for his father, but his voice came back at him flat and dull and scared.

Call the police.

But what could they do? It was too soon for Dad to be officially missing. They'd call at the house and speak to Ben before conducting a cursory search through the streets in their patrol car. By then, Dad might be dead.

Adrenaline stirred his blood, leaving his limbs spongy and frail. The taste of acid on his tongue and a knot in his throat. His eyes watered. He stared at the floor next to his feet until the chirrup of his phone startled him, and he took it from his pocket. His father's number.

Ben pressed 'answer' and held the phone to his head.

"Hello? Dad?"

Silence. Then, breathing, like from a throat packed with rags. A dry wheeze and bad air tasted on cardboard lips.

"Ben. Ben. Listen. Listen to me. Come out and find me in the fields. Please come and find me, lad. In the fields."

"Dad, what're you doing out there? Come home. Please."

"Listen, Ben. Come out and find me."

"Dad."

The line went dead.

"Dad."

Ben stared at the phone until his fingers turned numb and the glow faded from the screen.

Twelve

There was no answer when he called his father's number, and he only ended the call when the low battery warning flashed upon the screen. He placed it back in his pocket then set out for the fields and whatever waited for him out there among the stunted trees and slopes of Somerset dirt.

~

Into the fields, the perpetual dark, and the stars burned slow and patient like immortal hearts. Ben walked, searching in silence, pushing away the imagined movement at the limits of the torchlight. The sounds of night animals, their wails and plaintive calls, slipped across the countryside like low winds. The cold numbed his legs and crept up his spine like a surgeon's hands. The ground had dried since the last rainfall, but underneath the top soil the earth was soft and damp, and heavier feet than his would have sunk through.

His heart fluttered, jumped and unravelled as he moved through fallow fields. Across the low hills and flat land, trees were nothing more than memorial shadows spreading towards the sky. The distant fields were ghost shapes through the veil of another world far removed from the one he walked in.

His respiration and heartbeat conspired to deafen him, and he pretended not to hear the disconcerting voices on the breeze and distant calls across the slopes and rundown fields.

~

Ahead of Ben, a man was kneeling towards him in the dirt, head bowed and nodding slightly. Naked save for a pair of dampened boxer shorts.

Ben froze.

The man looked up, winced at the torchlight in his face, his hands upon his pot belly. His arms were scrawny and sallow. Oily black hair smeared over his brow above shoulders pointed and thin like a clothes hanger. A hawkish face mottled with small, dark bruises. The cold was upon him, shaking at his joints and sinew.

"Here you are," the man said, each word muttered merrily past mahogany teeth. "Have you had bad dreams, my friend?"

Ben's mouth opened then closed, gulping cold air like a fish stolen from the water. His thoughts floundered.

The man rose to his feet and skittered off into the dark, out of sight. Ben looked at the ground. Looked at his shaking hands. This was where he'd collapsed.

Where Doyle had found him. And now he imagined the ground to be spoiled and putrid under his feet, blackened and dire, a rotten quagmire littered with bones and mangy pelts.

He dabbed his eyes with the heels of his hands and inhaled deeply through a mouth that felt like frayed cloth and tasted of brine. A tremble passed over and through his arms. Nerve endings itched. He didn't want to collapse again; he didn't want to fall down and be found by those who walked the fields.

A light flared on the opposite side of the field. Ben turned. A fire had ignited, flames licking at the dark like errant limbs. It was a bonfire, calling him towards it.

Fear crept from his stomach and spread into the clammy, soft parts of him. He had no choice but to answer the call.

~

Ben slipped the knife into one sweat-greased hand. The muscles of his heart twinged and tightened. A cold dampness on his back, underneath his clothes, and he walked in little steps like a shameful child expecting rebuke. The bonfire was a nest of animated flames that bloomed like alien flowers. He was transfixed by its dance like a moth drawn to the light. The fire was hard to look away from. Tendrils of flame grasped for a sky it could never reach.

Dwarfed by its size, Ben stood before the bonfire like a supplicant seeking favour. The flames reached ten feet high; the base was at least six feet wide and made of branches, sticks and detritus scavenged from the land. His skin cringed from the heat that agitated the hairs on the back of his hands. His eyes stung as he stared into the fire and the flaming wood, and he pushed away the thought that his father had served as kindling. Flecks of ash settled on his face. Splinters of orange, yellow and deep red were so many glowing embers. Squalls of flame. Ben looked for bones among the raging heart of the fire. He retreated until the heat was less oppressive and he could take in a breath without scraping his throat raw.

A man appeared from behind the bonfire, a shadow melting from shadows, tall and thin and white-faced. A phantom clad in a long coat opened at the front. A clerical collar at the figure's throat. The man stepped around to Ben's side of the fire, and stood with his back to it, facing him.

"Hello, Ben." He knew that voice.

Being backlit by the fire darkened the man's features so that Ben couldn't discern any detail. He shone the torch at the man's face.

Reverend Glass smiled under white face paint that covered him from chin to hairline. His hair was slicked back from his brow. The white paint defined the sharp points of his face. Corpse-pallor. He looked taller with the fire behind him, framing his body with gouts of red flames.

"What brings you out here?" Glass said.

Ben tried to keep his body still, but the muscles in his face twitched and his legs were like saplings ready to fold. He glanced to his flanks and registered several figures either side of him, white-faced and watching intently. Suggestions of spindly bodies preparing for busy work. There was a lamenting cry from far away.

"I'm looking for my father," Ben said, hating how scared and small his voice was.

Glass grinned without teeth.

"Where's my father?" Ben said, aware of the knife, as light as a glass shard, and the damage it could do to soft flesh and skin. But the thought of using it on someone, cutting and opening meat that wasn't meant to be opened, turned his stomach to liquid.

Glass glanced at the knife; if he was worried he didn't show it. "Why are you really out here, Ben? Are you seeking reassurance or comfort? Are you lost? Are you looking to be found?"

"Do you know where my dad is?"

Another smile from the reverend, creasing the dried paint around his mouth and forming spider-web cracks under his eyes.

"You need help, Ben. You need communion."

"Just tell me where my dad is."

The fire crackled and clicked behind Glass. "That's not important at the moment."

"What have you done to him?"

"Victor is in good hands. He's safe. He's opened his eyes. You should too, Ben, because there is no other way. The world will be a very different place, very soon."

"I don't care about communion," Ben said. "I just want my dad."

"I'm here to help you, Ben," said Glass. "Let me help you."

"I don't want your help."

"That's not for you to decide. Something is coming for all of us, every man, woman and child. And we will share communion with it. You've dreamt of it, haven't you? You've dreamt of being lost in the darkness between worlds and the things that dwell there. There are gods out there, Ben. Something will be born into this world, and we will join with it."

Ben stepped back and almost tripped on a frozen ridge of ground. "I thought you only believed in your one god?"

Glass shook his head like he was shrugging off a bad joke. "I've come to realise it's a false god. A rumour told around desert campfires by shepherds and goat-herders. I believe in a god that dwells in the howling void and the gaps between realities. The black star. This world is covered by a skin that separates it from others, and in places the skin is worn and thin. And in other places the skin is torn and bleeding. The area around here is one such place where the skin is peeling and soon to be opened like a weeping wound. We are waiting for the black star to emerge."

"The black star," Ben said, remembering his dream. He wanted to turn and run, flee from madness and the worship of terrible things. But he would not turn away. He would not turn his back to the reverend.

"Are you unwell?" Glass asked him. "Are you hurt? Does your wife's disappearance still gnaw at you?"

"Don't talk about her," said Ben.

"You can be healed, Ben. Through communion. Communion with a god newly-born to this world."

"How do you know it's a god?" Ben's guts churned as he remembered his dream about being consumed by something immense and alien.

"Come with me," Glass said. "I can help you. I can clear away your confusion and fear. The black star will show you."

"Through communion."

"Yes. The black star wants us all."

"No thanks."

"You don't know what you'll be missing. It'll be wonderful."

"Is my dad here somewhere? Just tell me – then you can carry on with your mad fucking worship."

"Your father is safe."

"Then let me see him."

"Only if you come with me."

Ben held up the knife and its glinting blade. His intentions were clear, although he didn't know if he could follow them through to the end; to take the breath from a man's body and stop his heart. He wasn't made for murder.

Glass shook his head, disappointed. He cleared his throat. His eyes were sombre and serious. "I'm beyond death and pain. Beyond all the frivolous matters of this world. Our lives are a forgotten song. Our dreams are fodder for greater appetites. We are no more than primitive things scurrying through the dirt, and we should know our place. We are barely-evolved apes that made the mistake of looking into the void."

The fire made fluid shadows around Glass and gave the appearance of spindly insect appendages sprouting from his back. His shadow bled from his feet, stick-thin and loping as though it was reaching for Ben's neck.

"Just tell me where my father is," Ben said. "No more nonsense. I don't care about your fucking god."

"You should be honoured," Glass said. "This place will be ground zero, the site of emergence. The walls are thin here, and if you listen carefully you can hear the pulsing of other worlds."

Ben stepped towards the other man, the knife held by his waist. Glass made no attempt to dissuade him. Then there were grunts and cackles and yips and shouts out in the dark, and Ben turned towards them.

When he turned back, Glass was gone and part of the darkness, again. But he could be heard, not far away, no more than several feet. A low, soft voice taunting Ben.

The noises from the dark stopped. The silence shocked him. He looked around, frantic and scared, muttering under his breath, the blade of the knife pointed at the empty spaces before him. The fire raged, full of hurt and bluster. Then Glass stepped into the light, and Ben was between him and the bonfire. The heat behind him tightened the skin on the back of his head and coaxed sweat from his pores.

Glass held something in his arms; something like a pale infant wrestled from the innards of some swollen marine animal, swaddled in loose skin and dripping bits. Ben had to look twice to be certain of the thing cradled to Glass's chest. It was one of the jellyfish creatures, like the one Doyle had found a few days ago. Glistening and white-limbed. Tendrils hanging from Glass's arms. It was dead.

Glass smiled at Ben then looked down at the creature, his face flushed and full like a proud father. His eyes were glassy and too wide.

"It's beautiful, isn't it?" His hands, sleeves and the front of his clothes were wet.

Ben said nothing.

The jellyfish-thing twitched in Glass's hands. Ben started, the knife flinching in his hand.

"Don't worry," said Glass. "It's dead, I assure you. Just nerve endings firing one last time. Don't be afraid, Ben. They're not here to hurt us; they're heralds. They show the way for what comes after them. They are prey for larger appetites which empty worlds of life. They show the way for the black star."

Glass bowed his head towards the creature and bit down on one of its tendrils. The wet quiver in his mouth made Ben feel sick. Glass applied his jaws. Closed his eyes. A soft moan through a full mouth. The suck of lips upon wet meat. Then a crunch, like teeth biting into an apple, only wetter, more sopping.

"Christ," Ben said. He stepped too close to the fire and winced at the heat upon the backs of his legs.

Glass took the mouthful and began chewing, and his eyes opened and rolled into the back of his head so they resembled spiders' eggs. A shiver of pleasure. He savoured the alien flesh. Milky fluid spilled around his mouth and down his chin. The bitten tendril wept to the dirt. Glass dropped the creature, and it hit the ground like the bag of a butcher's throwaway cuttings. A stink of ammonia and rotting vegetation. Glass held his hands to his face. His shoulders trembled and he hunched over, stricken by the potency of the creature's blood. His arms were trembling and stiffened, and from his mouth came a low whisper like tall grass stirred by a breeze. Ben thought he heard a small, almost child-like, laugh from the man.

Put the knife into his gut, a voice told Ben. *Stab and kill. Finish it.*

Glass straightened. His face was waxen and sharp. The glazed eyes of a junkie.

Ben felt the world stagger and his vision caper. The roar of the fire was all around him, the ground was uneven underneath his feet, the moon above was uncaring, and he was a distressed animal caught among them all. His legs wilted. His vision faded and then returned, but the world didn't feel the same.

And then Glass was beside him, one hand upon his arm, and muttering in his ear. Muttering all sorts of things.

"I can see through the veil," Glass whispered. His

breath smelled like mildewed walls and damp corners of wood and dirt. Corruption in his mouth like black rot. "I can see what waits for us, Ben, once we share communion. The black star. You have to see the black star. It wants to meet us all." A deep, shuddering breath was taken past the puckered rim of his pale lips, and Glass muttered an unknown dialect that sounded like nothing Ben had ever heard. A dead language given life by Glass's dancing tongue. Those unknown words made Ben feel sick and woozy.

Around them, other bonfires rose from the ground in gouts and small geysers of flame. The field was alight with a hundred fires of all sizes and statuesque figures with white faces.

Glass grinned; his white face cracked and creased.

Ben stumbled from the reverend's hands and ran. Glass called after him and was lost among the fires.

Thirteen

Ben fled from the field of bonfires, into the moonlit dark where he glimpsed people with faces painted milk-white and morose, cruel and unforgiving. A man scarred with arcane symbols capered at the periphery of his swaying vision. Unknown, runic shapes and opened skin. Dried blood and chattering teeth. Ben ran blindly, the torchlight bobbing before his stumbling feet. He spat breath from his raw throat and deflated lungs. His eyes watered from bonfire smoke as he glimpsed candlelight within the woods. A herd of grazing deer scattered from his approach and melted into the treeline.

The torchlight and the muted moonlight showed him things he would never forget:

A naked woman writhed, endorphin-high, as she was enveloped by the twisting limbs of a jellyfish. Their bodies merged and flesh conflated, wet skin and dripping fluid. A glistening smile was the last thing Ben saw of her face before her head was lost to the pawing of maggot-white tendrils.

A man-like figure wearing the mask of an antlered stag emerged from deep shadow and made mewling noises through a dusty mouth.

A boy was crouched over something wet at his

feet, wiping his mouth with small fingers. When the torchlight danced over him and made his eyes gleam, he screamed and shrilled like something caught in a steel trap.

Ben glanced back and saw moving shapes thrilled by the chase, yipping and calling to him. Laughter from white-faced devils and black-eyed angels. Caterwauls echoed around the low hills. He turned off the torch in the hope they would lose him and kicked his legs harder even as he sobbed at the pain shooting up his thighs. The lights of the village seemed so distant they could have been out to sea. He ignored the tightening in his knees. He could only go deeper into the fields.

Human figures wailed at his flanks, loping over the hard ground. A grunted cry to his right that was too close, and he flailed instinctively in that direction. A white face emerged and grinned at him, all slack and elastic.

Ben staggered wheezing through hedgerows, climbing over sagging wooden fences. He hauled himself over awkward stiles. At one point he stumbled and fell, and sprawled on the ground with a mouthful of mouldering grass and the smell of animal spoor upon him. His legs were all pain and heat. The air left his lungs as though it had been pulled out. Footfalls, cracking sticks, and the sound of leaves disturbed by slapping feet were getting closer. Part of him simply wanted to stay on the ground with his elbows mired in the dirt and wait for them to find his shivering form. To lie under a full moon and let the hands of madmen fall on him.

Ben crawled into a ditch and lay among frigid nettles and thorns. He held his breath against the stench of badger urine and slow rot. He closed his eyes as quick footsteps came from nearby then slowed as they approached the ditch and became silent. Ben didn't move. Thorns pierced the legs of his trousers and sunk their needle tips into his skin. Beetles scurried around and over him. Something tiny and chirping dug its fangs into the soft meat of his cheek. He gritted his teeth, opened his eyes. He could sense *them* just beyond the ditch, and when he peered over the rim of the ditch there were vague outlines of bodies and alabaster faces turned towards the moon. A murmured voice and a sniffling sigh. Leathery click of tendons and ligaments. A child's giggle.

He looked away and imagined them creeping towards him, smelling his stink and fear. He didn't want to die in a ditch.

But then he heard them move away, their footfalls receding until the only sounds were the rustling of mice in the grass. He dragged himself from the ditch and shook away all kinds of scuttling and slithering things. There was such a temptation to slouch back into the ditch with the crawling insects and piercing thorns that he almost laughed from the hysteria climbing his insides. He looked up at the sky and the burning stars, those shards of heaven. There was something different about the sky, and he didn't know if it was real or imagined or the manifestation of concentrated insanity from the fields below it.

He remembered the unknown constellations he'd witnessed from the back garden.

Stepping back, he gasped. The sky was a tumult of alien colours and shadows, and within them a black hole gaped and turned. Falling stars and corpse-lights. The death of the universe in fire and heat, ice and oblivion. And from within it all, a presence emerged from behind the thinnest of veils, bulging and pawing against something that looked like a membrane that could cover an ocean. Waiting to be born into this world.

Then it faded from the sky like a bad dream suddenly forgotten. Ben blinked black roses from his eyes.

The stars returned. He ran.

~

The old woman appeared as he hunched over to regain his breath. Ben switched on the torch to reveal her, and then wished he hadn't. She was naked, and between her legs was a crest of feathery white hair around a glistening, raw, grey-lipped slit with red insides. Her awful flower. Ben cried out and she was upon him before he could move away, shambling like a crumpled marionette, all dry and flapping. Her fingers became busy at Ben's belt. The breath she coughed into his face was like sour milk and yeast. Her body held the reek of bad wine and steaming mince. He pushed her and backed away, tripped and fell onto his backside.

She lunged for him, pouncing upon his legs and grabbing them with swollen paws. She fell to her knees and Ben felt his stomach plummet when he looked into her face.

It was the old woman from the shop, Sally, who he'd comforted in that cold backroom.

She lowered her head, and Ben screamed at the sheer horror of her puckering mouth at his crotch, nuzzling him with her squirming tongue and ratty teeth. On his thigh, he could feel the dampness between her legs. Ben drew strength into his back and heaved her away, and she rolled onto her side. He pulled himself up and staggered away from her keening form, noticing with a cry of relief that Doyle's house was in the distance, squat against the horizon.

Guttural laughter echoed across the fields, gaining on him. He was slowing, hobbling, trying to wipe the musk of the old woman from his body. Sweat dripped in his eyes, turning the world watery and vague. Darkness at his flanks and his front and back. He tripped, fell to his knees, got up, and kept moving. The sound of chattering mouths getting closer, closer, closer all the time. Burning lungs, legs and heart. Hot skin. A deep stitch in his side slowed him to walking pace.

Doyle's house wasn't far away but the windows were dark. Ben let out a low, mournful sob. His stomach folded and he spat bile down his front. He raised his face and the sky seemed alive, churning, cascading. Trampling feet behind him, nearly upon him. He didn't look back. Didn't want to look back. He didn't want to see the face of whoever was breathing excitedly so close behind him. He scaled a low fence and fell down. No time to look back or examine the grazes on his palms as he stumbled towards the house. He sagged against the garden gate, and when he opened it he looked over his shoulder to see the villagers bolting towards him across the open ground.

Into the garden, where he was blinded by a sudden light which turned the immediate world around him white and stained the lawn with his shadow. He held one hand against his face and peered through the bars of his fingers. Security lights. The windows of the house were still dark.

Don't stop.

And then he was banging and punching at the front door, calling for Doyle to let him in. His palms stung. He tried the handle but it would only turn so far, and the door didn't move from its jamb.

The creak of the garden gate behind him. He turned slowly, flinching at what he thought he might see.

The villagers lurked at the garden threshold, their white faces like dead moons. Eyes that were dry slits, rimmed with pink, squinty and mottled. Creased mouths and dirty clothes. Hands that curled and uncurled, damp-palmed and twitching. They bobbed their heads and hitched their shoulders. Bruises on their throats. Whispered his name as they wiped their mouths.

"Ben, Ben, Ben," they said, with something like fervour and joy in their voices. *"Ben, Ben, Ben..."*

He slumped against the door and called out for Doyle. He shouted as the villagers took small measured steps down the cracked path. His chest felt like it was collapsing. He fell into a sitting position, his back against the hard door. His legs wouldn't move despite his efforts, and his knees were like white-hot slag. Exhaustion left him crippled and sobbing as he waited for the villagers, with their vile mouths and gleaming faces, to take him. Take him back to the fields.

They came for him on well-heeled shoes, boots and trainers.

The door opened behind him. Light from inside the house. The smell of paint-thinner, oil colours and sweat. Ben fell back onto a pair of old boots. He looked up at Doyle and opened his mouth, but nothing came out.

The dog was growling. Bared teeth. Muscled legs trembling.

Doyle shouldered a hunting rifle. He worked the bolt, looked down the black barrel. The villagers halted, filling the pathway and beyond the gate. Doyle stepped over Ben's prone body and on to the path. "I know who you all are! I see you all! Mary Browning, John Woodley, Craig Falk, Dennis Hymes, Susan Little, Tom Malone, Jenny Malone, Nathan Lark, Margaret Hill, Emma Hewitt! I know you all! Leave! Leave now!"

The wolfhound barked and growled, keeping pace at Doyle's side. The villagers retreated from the rifle, into the dark beyond the light, until all that could be seen was the pale wash of their faces and the fading gleam of small eyes as they melted away.

Ben sagged in the doorway.

The dog lumbered back and licked at Ben's face. He closed his eyes and squirmed at the rough tongue across his brow. He could only complain weakly and wave one hand at the dog.

Doyle came back up the pathway. Ben looked up at him, mouth agape, eyes stinging. Doyle grabbed him by the arms and pulled him inside the house.

Fourteen

With a blanket over his trembling shoulders Ben stared at the floor, wishing to sink into the armchair and be absorbed into the fabric, stitching and old foam. He drank hot tea from a mug cradled in his fingers as he tried not to agitate his scraped palms. His insides were like defrosting meat sloshing in a bag. He couldn't think straight and his addled brain pulsed hotly while lactic acid turned his limbs brittle and heavy.

Doyle had locked the door and now kept watch from a window. The dog sat by his feet, ears twitching at distant sounds. Doyle occasionally glanced back at Ben and watched him without expression.

Ben shivered, ignoring the paintings of monsters and old gods upon the walls. Madness was creeping into his mind, colouring the world in stark light. He called his father's phone and let it ring to voicemail, where he left a message of quiet words and desperation. Then he put the phone away, certain that he would never talk to his father again.

Doyle retreated from the window and sat on the wooden chair across from Ben. He stood the rifle against the wall then grabbed the vodka bottle by the skirting board and tipped it into his mouth. He drank it like water, and when he was done he wiped his mouth with the back of one tattooed arm. Ben flicked his eyes towards the man and finished the last dregs of his tea.

Doyle tossed the bottle to him. "Get it down you. You need it." He chased the vodka with a can of energy drink from his jacket pocket.

Ben said nothing, unscrewed the cap and wiped the mouth of the bottle, then drank.

"I don't think they're coming back," said Doyle. "They're keeping their distance. If they come near the house again, we'll know."

Ben nodded, the muscles slack in his face.

"Bad night out in the dark," Doyle continued. "What were you doing out there?"

"Looking for my father. I woke up and he was gone from the house. I searched the village, but couldn't find him. Then he called me from his phone and told me to find him in the fields." Ben took a long hit from the bottle and grimaced. "I didn't find him. But I found other things."

He told Doyle what he had found.

"Reverend Glass," Doyle said. "I thought so. He's the leader of their little cult, if that's what you can call it. All the people who've been corrupted by the dreams."

"They want communion," said Ben. "Glass

mentioned something called 'the black star'." He paused. "I've dreamt of the black star."

"Yeah, I thought you had," Doyle said, nodding. "The cult is preparing the way for its arrival. Not that it'll save them. Or the rest of us."

They passed the bottle back and forth between them.

"The end of all things," Ben said, and his words seemed unreal. He had a strong urge to scratch at his skin and study what was underneath.

Doyle was silent.

"I can't leave my dad out there," said Ben.

Doyle looked at the floor. "If he's with Glass and the others it's already too late. Just accept it."

"I can't."

"You can't go out there and look for him again while it's still dark. The cult is outside, waiting for us to come out; for *you* to come out. They want more dreamers."

"I can't just stay here and get drunk."

"You will, if you've got any sense."

"Fuck off."

"What makes you think you'll find your father if you go out there again? And what if you find him and he's not the man he once was? How will you deal with that?"

Ben wanted to move, to lift his legs and stand, but his body felt like it was weighed down by stones and pebbles. He was terrified. If he gave in to the pressure in his eyes, the tears would fall down his face in thin streams. He was a twisted thing of rags and skin with a rabbit's juddering heart.

"Stay here," said Doyle. "It's for the best."

"For the best," Ben muttered, and he was shocked at how reedy and insipid his voice was. "Christ."

Distant laughter echoed from outside, and both men looked towards the front of the house. The dog raised its head and growled.

The laughter died.

Doyle eased back on his chair and cracked his knuckles. "What did your father tell you about me?"

"He said you were in the army once. Something about an accident."

"Not far from the truth."

"Yeah?"

"Yeah."

Ben looked at him. "Go on."

Fifteen

"I was in Afghanistan. 2005. Blair and Bush's clusterfuck. Infantry. There'd been reports of strange weather patterns and the remains of unknown animals found near a small Pashtun village in Kandahar province. Reports from local men that their families were having bad dreams about unknown lands and demons. Tales of people going missing. One of the local shepherds said he'd been having visions of the stars changing to constellations he didn't recognise."

"Bloody hell," said Ben.

"The top brass were worried that insurgents were conducting raids from within the village or using it to test a chemical weapon of some kind. My unit was sent in to find out what was going on." Doyle paused, shifted on the chair.

"So what happened?" Ben asked.

"We entered the village, expecting trouble, but the streets were deserted. Complete silence. I had expected an ambush, at least, but as we moved deeper into the village no one was there to stop us. Then a man came stumbling out of a ramshackle hut, his arms raised. He was gaunt, trembling and exhausted. From what our translator told us, he said that everyone else was at the mosque in the centre of the village – I could its minaret peering over the houses. The man was crying as he spoke. Looked like he hadn't slept for days, and stank of old piss. He said that all his family had gone to the mosque. Everyone had painted their faces white. He sank to his knees and pleaded with us to kill him, to spare him from his fate.

"We arrived at the mosque minutes later. I was in the squad that went in. The villagers were lying on the floor of the main hall – over a hundred of them, men, women and children – and most of them were dead; the rest were dying. Looked like they had all decided to just lie down and die. We moved among them, stepping carefully, in case it was some kind of trap. Some of them had been bleeding from their noses, mouths and ears. Glazed, dull eyes. The great room smelled of ammonia and shit. Some of the villagers had soiled themselves."

"At the centre of the hall, the local imam was gasping for air and sobbing. He started babbling at us. Our translator told us what he was saying: *It promised us communion. The black star.*" Then the imam said that there was a sudden burning light and a deafening ringing. We had no idea what he meant.

"We called in medics and administered help to the dying people, but we couldn't do much for them.

Then something happened. There was a ringing sound, mixed with faint animal cries. The air smelled worse.

"I saw the air shimmer behind Corporal Grady, like a rising heat wave. And then there was a blinding light and a sound like a hundred screaming mouths. Before I could react, it was happening all around me. The hall seemed to tilt and sway. There was weapons fire. Men panicked. Shouts and screams. Chatter on my radio. It felt like the air was moving, like water, and the hall went dark, only lit by gunfire. I saw the screaming faces of my mates. And then I was running. I'd dropped my rifle. Me and Jed Wainwright were the only survivors of the squad sent into the mosque. I can't remember anything after that. Later, I was told that when we ran outside we were crying. Jed had lost his rifle, too. When another squad was sent in to investigate, they found no trace of the other soldiers. My mates. All gone. Snuffed out of existence. Only the dead villagers on the floor remained."

Doyle sunk a mouthful of vodka. His face seemed drawn inwards. Dark in his eyes. He didn't look at Ben.

"What happened to you afterwards?" said Ben.

"Me and Jed were taken to a military hospital and checked over. We were mostly lucid, I think. I remember being examined by a stern-faced doctor with cold hands and coffee-breath. I was questioned by my superiors. So many fucking questions. The nights afterwards were filled with bad dreams and awful nightmares. Hallucinations. Just over a month later, Jed hung himself. My superiors gave me the option to leave the army, and I took it. I couldn't go back out there. Not again. I got a decent pension out of it, probably to keep me quiet. I heard that the village was bombed, wiped from the face of the earth. The families of the other soldiers were told that the men died in an explosion that had vaporised their bodies. In the following years I had intermittent dreams of holes in our world and glimpses of other worlds and dimensions. All the things I've painted..."

Ben swallowed against the dryness in his throat. "So, in the mosque, the imam said that something went wrong. What did he mean?"

"It seems obvious now," Doyle said. "I only just realised yesterday, when I saw the full horror of the black star in a dream, like you did, and it whispered to me its plans for us. I discovered that it wanted to enter our world, like it'd tried to do in Afghanistan nearly a decade ago, when something had gone wrong and it couldn't break through. I can't believe it took so long for me to realise what the imam was talking about. I've been so stupid. Maybe I was just in denial. A part of me thought that they had simply gathered to worship in the mosque and had poisoned themselves in some sort of mass suicide, and that I had hallucinated the rest. Or maybe whatever had happened in that mosque was due to hallucinogenic aerosols in the air or something that altered our perception. I almost convinced myself. I wasn't even sure something was wrong until I found the jellyfish in the field and noticed people in Marchwood acting strange. And when I dreamt of the black star, I finally realised what it wanted and how terrible it is."

Ben said, "So why didn't it emerge into our world back then?"

Doyle shook his head and bit his lip. "Maybe we just got lucky, in that respect. A quirk of fate. It was nothing we did. Maybe the stars weren't right."

"So we might get lucky again?" Ben said. "The black star might not be able to emerge?"

"I doubt it. Not again."

"We can't stop it then? All we can do is wait and hide?"

"Hiding won't do you any good. It's the end of all things."

"I can't believe that. I refuse to believe that."

"It's only going to get worse," said Doyle. "We're past the tipping point. It's only a matter of time before the skin of this world tears, and whatever the entity is will emerge like a newborn into this world.

And then it's going to get very, very bad. We, as a species, will not survive contact with the black star. It's beyond anything we've ever encountered. Beyond anything that's ever lived on this planet. Its presence will crush our minds."

Ben held his heads in his hands. Frantic thoughts circled his skull. The endless dark of extinction. When he looked up at Doyle, the man was scratching absently at one wrist.

"How long until it arrives?" Ben said. He thought of all the children and babies in the world, and his heart dropped into his stomach.

Doyle glanced at him. Red-rimmed eyes. "A few days, at most. Glass's group have prepared the way for it. This has been coming for a long time. Now our time is up, my friend."

"A few days. Christ."

Doyle snorted. "Jesus won't help us now."

"If you suspect that the black star is coming, why haven't you already left?" said Ben. "Why haven't you fled up north or across the Channel? If this island is doomed, then why are you still here?"

The suggestion of a thin, wan smile at Doyle's grim mouth. "This is my home. The land I was born upon. Even if I did run, it would only delay the inevitable. Once the black star's here its influence will spread. It'll absorb all life. This will be ground zero. I'm supposed to be here, to witness the end. I may just stay home with Fenrir and a bottle of vodka, wait and see what'll happen. I may end up in another place, in another time, for all I know."

"You're not going to do anything?" said Ben. "You're just going to accept it?"

"Nothing else to be done, Ben. We're just meat and skin. Screaming ganglia and nerve endings. What would you propose we do? Spread around some holy water and pray?"

"You won't help me find my father?"

"He's gone," said Doyle. "You can go out there and look for him, if you like. But I'd wait until first light, if I were you. And even then I'm not sure you'd be safe out there. The corrupted ones have added to their ranks, and they will continue to do so until their god arrives. You might be one of them by tomorrow, Ben."

"It's not fair. It's not right." Tears brimmed in Ben's eyes and the floor seemed to drop away from him.

"If it helps," said Doyle. "It'll all be over soon."

Sixteen

The birds in the trees were silent.

First light and cold air. Puddles of ice like dirty mirrors. Frost on the ground, crackling under Ben's feet as he picked his way from the fields into the village. He struggled under the bleeding white sky and imagined snow falling upon a silent, dead world years from now.

The main street through the village was deserted. Recycling wheelie bins had fallen on their sides. He passed an empty child's pushchair on the pavement. A dog was barking in a nearby garden.

As he trudged past the church he glimpsed figures flitting between the graves.

Past the open front doors of silent houses. Not far from his father's house, he stopped in the middle of the road and stared at his upturned palms, which were red and sore. He doubted his reality, his life, and the structures around him. Even the ground under his feet. Maybe it was an existence of illusion to stay ignorant of the teeming darkness outside this world. He wondered if this was the last morning he'd ever see. The last morning anyone would ever see.

He was exhausted and miserable, an

amalgamation of weak bones, tired meat and blind networks of nerve endings and veins. Blood moved slowly through his body. His heartbeat was heavy and slow.

Folk music was coming from one of the houses. It sounded distant, ethereal, and halfway out of this world.

The music followed him all the way to his father's house.

~

The door was unlocked. Ben entered the house, cowed from the silence around him. The threat of ambush leaked from shadows and corners. His leaden footsteps were too loud. Dirty shoeprints on the kitchen linoleum. He stood in the house of slanted rooms and cold walls, surrounded by shadows of his childhood. Lost years. Shades of his mother and the things she left behind.

The living room appeared undisturbed from how he'd left it last night. He saw his own reflection in the television screen, and it was gaunt and lumpy, haggard and bowed, a ghost made of sticks and stones.

Ben looked out at the back garden and froze. His shoulders slumped. Hysterical laughter bloomed in his chest.

Dad was standing in the garden, a crumpled shape staring at the sky.

~

Ben walked out to the garden and stood next to his father, whose clothes were clean but smelled of leaf-mulch and brambles. The back of the old man's neck under his collar was damp. Greased hair and scalp, as if he'd been running under the boughs of dripping trees. His face was cleaved by a distracted smile as he stared at the sky, and his eyes were wide and watery, full of revelation and awe. He didn't look at Ben.

"Beautiful morning, isn't it, lad?"

Ben looked at the side of his father's face and noticed the slow tick at the corner of his left eye. "Where did you go last night?"

His father closed his eyes as his smile faltered. "Things have changed, son."

"I know that, Dad. The black star."

"Yes."

"Tell me more."

"I can show you. Come with me."

"Where?"

His father turned to him as crows flocked from the slated roofs of houses and screamed overhead. "Everything will be revealed."

~

They walked through the village in silence. A few people wandered the streets, walking their dogs or leaving for work. A car exhaust choked and spat. Ben kept glancing at his father, checking for a zipper at the back of his neck or the edge of a rubber mask blended into the skin under his jawline.

"Why don't we just leave the village, Dad? We'll get in my car and drive away. There's no need to stay."

"We can't do that. Not now. You don't understand, Ben."

Tired parents dropped their kids off at the primary school. Uniforms and small rucksacks were bursts of colour upon the grey road, but there were no smiles, and the rest of the world was all fading shadows. The children were quiet as they walked through the school's front doors. A teacher stood by the entrance and smiled at each child who passed her.

Dad stopped at the entrance to the graveyard. "This way, my lad."

Ben looked up at the church spire.

"They're waiting for us," said Dad.

"I don't want to, Dad," Ben said.

His father gently touched his shoulder. "This is the only way. Do this for me. Please."

Ben shook his head and looked at the ground to avoid the oily gleam in Dad's eyes. But he went into the churchyard and walked down the stone path at his father's side, a loyal son to the last, a bewildered heart waiting for the end.

Seventeen

The great doors opened, and his father led him inside. Ben followed hesitantly, fighting the urge to turn and run as he was enfolded by the stone walls and the freezing floor.

Burning candles and the smell of incense, and something foul and ripe beneath that, like perfume sprayed over fruiting bodies. The candles offered little light against the swathes of darkness in far corners and high nooks.

They halted ten yards inside the church.

Dad placed one hand on Ben's arm.

A large congregation waited for them in the pews. Rows of unmoving bodies faced the front, where the spindly figure of Reverend Glass was standing, meek and mild and terribly unassuming.

The congregation turned and stared at Ben, approximately a hundred of them, men and women and children, dressed in their Sunday bests. Floral dresses under soft coats. Tweed jackets over knotted shoulders. Dark blazers and waistcoats that restricted bulbous stomachs and fatty biceps. Long skirts with stained lace hems and laddered black stockings. Their faces were painted white, and some grinned at him, keepers of a special secret; others scowled or frowned, wary of him. The man sitting nearest to Ben cleared something wet from his throat. A woman tittered from under the splayed hand upon her lips.

The congregation had grown in the last days. He recognised some of them; the pub landlord, the butcher, and the pregnant woman who lived across the road. And despite their barely restrained fervour, the villagers were gaunt-faced and sore-eyed. Mouths were wiped by shaking hands. A handkerchief on the floor with a spot of blood upon it. Scratch marks on the backs of hands and arms. Lesions on necks and throats. Bad teeth and damp lips. Cold sores. A boy with a cleft palate drooled onto his chin. Old people with false teeth and gleaming gums curling in a smile. The faint smell of sickness and neglect steamed from their bodies. They were twitching, fiddling with their limbs, a gathering of insects in a nest.

"Welcome," said Reverend Glass, his voice carrying down the aisle. He gestured for Ben and his father to approach the front.

Dad took Ben's hand and they went willingly to Glass, cleaving the sea of pale white faces.

~

Ben hadn't immediately realised, but the interior of the church had been altered. Christian symbols had been removed. The stained glass windows were smeared with oil and grease, and the old walls glistened with some sort of fluid. Charred Bibles, sloppily burnt, were piled in one corner. Esoteric symbols had been drawn upon the stone columns and pillars holding up the roof. The slopping corpses of the jellyfish-things were heaped upon and around the altar.

Ben and his father faced Glass at the front of the pews, watched by a captive audience. Behind Ben, fingers tapped on wood and low, snorted breaths tainted the air. He looked down at the stone floor and noticed pigeon feathers around his feet. He felt the weight of the congregation's attention on his back, a similar feeling to his wedding day all those years ago. The sudden thought of Emily made his chest ache.

The reverend's face, white and garish like a porcelain mask, was lit by the most awful of grins. His greased hair hung in tufts at the sides of his head and one side of his gouged mouth twitched moistly. Bloodshot eyes strained and bulged in their bone sockets. Despite the white paint covering his face, the skin was mottled with dark bruises. His lymph glands appeared swollen and pulsing.

"Have you come to join us, Ben?" Glass said. He crept closer and the grin didn't leave his face.

"I'm not here by choice," Ben said.

"There's always a choice."

"You had a choice?"

"Of course. I haven't been coerced; I'm here by free will."

"You've been brainwashed," said Ben. "All of you." He stared at his father until the older man looked away.

"You're very fortunate," said Glass. "We could have killed you last night. You have your father to thank for your reprieve. You were disrupting our preparations. But now you're here, willingly. You've accepted that the world is changing. Accept communion. Worship with us. There is no other way."

"The black star doesn't care about any of us," said Ben. "Even those who worship it. It'll kill us all."

Glass snorted. "You've been talking to Mr Doyle too much, Ben. He has no idea and no appreciation. But he will conform. He will join us soon. So will you."

Ben looked at his father. "Dad, you don't have to do this. We can leave the village. Please, Dad."

"You don't understand, Ben," his father said. "If you knew what waits for us and what will happen to us when the black star emerges and we embrace it, you'd accept without question. Communion. As one vessel."

"No, Dad. You're coming with me." He went to

grab his father's arm, but Glass stepped between them, hawkish and thin, and faced Ben.

"Get out of my way," Ben said. "Or I'll put you down. I promise."

Glass raised his hands. "Be calm, Ben. Think about what you're doing."

"I know what I'm doing. Get out of the way."

"You're tired and confused."

"I'm fine."

"You should sleep. You should dream. Dream of what awaits us."

"No." His shoulders slumped and he swallowed bile back down his throat.

"Close your eyes. We'll look after you."

"Fuck off."

Glass looked at the front row of the congregation. Those stark white faces leering and grinning. Then he nodded at Ben.

"Take him."

The front row rose in a hush of cloth and fabric and the scrape of worn heels on the floor. The chatter of anticipation. A stifled grunt and the creaking of dry limbs.

As numerous hands grasped and pawed at Ben, he pulled the knife from his coat and swiped at the air. The white faces and their musty-clothed bodies stepped back. A young man with a shaven head picked at his crusted lips with his fingers and stared at Ben.

One of the women opened her mouth at him and she was without teeth.

Ben grabbed Glass around the neck with his free hand so that he was stood behind the reverend with the knife to his throat. Glass's body under his overcoat and garments was like sticks and cold air. Those villagers who stood held their distance and glared at Ben with seething hot hatred.

"Back off," Ben said as a woman began creeping towards him. "I promise I'll cut his throat."

The woman halted, flinching and twitching. She sneered.

Glass struggled and shifted in Ben's hold. The reverend's skin felt like it was writhing.

His father looked at him with disappointed eyes. "You don't have to do this, Ben. Accept communion. Please."

"Listen to your father," Glass rasped.

"Shut the fuck up, Reverend."

Ben felt rather than saw Glass's mouth contort into a grin. "What are you going to do? It doesn't matter if you kill me. Another will take my place. This is futile, Ben. Stop it."

Ben looked at his father's unpainted face. "Come on, Dad. We're leaving."

The old man shook his head. "I can't, Ben. It's too late for that."

"It's not too late."

"It is." The frailty of his father's voice broke Ben's heart. "The black star is coming. Our new god is coming. Put the knife down and accept it."

"Dad!"

"No, son. No. If you have to leave, then leave. And remember that I still love you. But you won't survive this world once our god emerges."

Ben gritted his teeth against the welling of tears in his eyes. He knew his father was lost to him. "I'm sorry I couldn't help you, Dad."

His father nodded, wiped at his mouth, then turned away to face the altar and the glistening offerings upon it.

Ben backed away down the aisle, dragging Glass with him. The villagers rose from their seats, intent and watching. They wished him dead. Wished him in the ground or torn apart on a wooden cross.

Ben pressed the tip of the knife blade into Glass's skin. Glass was silent and compliant. When Ben reached the doors he pushed Glass away and stumbled outside. He shut the door behind him.

Snow was falling. He raised his face to the sky.

A gunshot rang out from across the road, followed by a moment of silence punctuated by the scrape of breath from his mouth. Then several more gunshots pierced the air and echoed like violent percussions.

Ben staggered down the path between the graves

and out onto the street, where he ran into groups of crying, screaming schoolchildren upon the road and between the parked cars. He quickly pocketed the knife. Teachers tried to control and organise the children into one group, holding the hands of the younger children, and take them down the road away from the school. Some children had blood on their clothes. They looked stunned and terrified, as though they'd just been pulled into a world unknown to them.

Another gunshot rang out from inside the school.

Ben wandered among the panicked crowd that filled the road. He pulled aside a wide-eyed young woman in a black skirt. Her face was trembling, her shoulders hitching with each strained sob through her mouth. She stared into his face. Saliva dampened her lips.

"He shot the children," she muttered. "He killed Mrs Chambers and Miss Bloom."

"Who did?"

She took a breath. "A tall, bearded man with tattoos. He walked into the classroom and just started shooting."

"Is anyone alive in there?"

She was shaking her head to wake herself from a bad dream. "I don't know. It happened so fast. We just tried to get the children out as quickly as we could. There was blood on the floor, and on the books and the walls. It sprayed. Did you know that? It sprayed everywhere."

Ben handed his phone to the woman. "Call the police."

Glassy-eyed, she looked at the phone like it had fallen from the sky. Her mouth opened and she nodded faintly, her face wan and freckled. Specks of snow landed on her hair and her shoulders.

He left her staring at the phone and crossed the road as the other teachers ushered the remaining children away from the school. He moved across the grassed area of bare trees and shrubs, and up the paved pathway to the entrance, grasping at his tightening chest. He had to get inside before he changed his mind and the strength drained from his legs.

The doors were open. A girl's red shoe lay on the steps leading up to the doorway. He drew the knife from his coat as the screams and cries behind him were muffled and turned to echoes by the falling snow.

Eighteen

A little girl slumped against the cloakroom wall, her face partly obscured by hanging coats, scarves, and satchels decorated with animal stickers. Long white socks reached up to her knees above shiny black shoes polished that morning. Blood pooled around her legs.

Ben pulled back the coats to reveal her opened eyes and round face below a mop of curly red hair. She had died with a frown on her face and a dark, wet wound in her stomach. Ben had to lean against the wall and screw his eyes shut. The urge to sob and shout nearly overwhelmed him.

"I'm sorry," he whispered as he bent towards her. His breath moved a strand of her hair. "I'm so sorry."

He left her where she rested and stepped into the first classroom, where the air smelled like burnt toast and Play-Doh. He tried to remember how the classroom looked when he had gone to school here over twenty-five years ago.

Everything changes. Nothing changes.

A table was overturned, metal legs pointing to the ceiling. Pencils, crayons, felt tip pens, and stationary littered the soft carpet. Knocked-over plastic chairs. A whiteboard of simple maths sums.

A broken abacus had spilled most of its counting beads, scattered like marbles. The walls were covered in the children's crude drawings of trees, fields, people and animals. Cartoon characters and Disney princesses. Dancing monkeys and pandas with false grins. Vivid shades of purple, yellow, green, blue and orange. And red. Lots of red. The smell of murder lingered like smoke. Bullet casings like a sprinkling of shiny trinkets.

A speckled trail of blood led to a dead boy on his side in one far corner, slack and white below a bookshelf. His hands were stained red and wet; he'd tried to stem the flow of blood from the bullet wound in his neck.

The wind sighed in the walls.

There were three more children on the other side of the room beneath the tall windows. A small bloody handprint on the wall. Two girls and another boy. Glistening exit wounds and crumpled limbs, open mouths frozen with the last breath out of their little lungs. Maybe they called for their mums and dads as they died. Maybe they didn't have time. It might have been thought of as cruel, but Ben hoped they didn't; he hoped they died quickly, without suffering, without the knowledge that they'd never eat ice cream or crisps or chocolate, or see their parents, ever again. Or feel the sun on their faces. Sleep in a warm bed. Never again for all those beloved things, because they had been taken by a man with a gun.

The smell of opened bodies made Ben dry heave in long, rasping sobs. Such despair. Mrs Chambers and Miss Bloom were sprawled in opposite corners, one of them atop a table with crayon drawings strewn beneath her. Ben's stomach flipped and dropped, and he swayed on legs that didn't feel like his own. He heaved again and, this time, he vomited pale fluid that landed by his feet and stained his shoes. He hunched over and regained his breath as he wiped his eyes. Where were the police? He should have heard sirens already. Armed response units and flashing blue lights should have been outside by now.

He stepped quietly into the next classroom, where the younger children had been taught. He hesitated, wincing, at the acrid, hot stench of urine, blood and gunpowder. Unfinished drawings of zebras and giraffes, and one of a child's pet dog. A potted plant spilled soil. Toy dinosaurs were discarded on the floor. He'd loved dinosaurs when he was a kid. Through the large windows at the top of the wall facing the street, he saw the snowfall growing heavier, and thought he could hear it pattering on the roof. His guts shrivelled as he stayed close to the wall and inched his way around, scanning the large room for bodies and bad surprises.

He almost slipped when he stepped on a yellow wax crayon that crumbled under his foot. He thought he could hear a low crying sound, as though its author was trying to stifle it through a smothering hand. On the floor were broken forms of children, and he didn't look for too long in case they opened their eyes and mouths to plead with him and demand to know why he hadn't saved them.

"I thought you would come here, Ben," a voice said from the other end of the classroom.

Ben didn't move from the wall.

Doyle was sat on a wooden stool in a darkened corner with the rifle barrel pointed under his chin. "You don't need the knife, Ben. I'm not going to hurt you. I'm done."

It took all of Ben's strength to step from the wall, and when he did he moved like a puppet with cut strings. The body of a blonde-haired girl lay between them, limbs twisted. Pigtails and pink wristbands.

"You shot those children, Doyle. Those teachers. You murdered them."

Doyle was shaking his head. Tears on his long beard. "No, I did it to save them. Don't you understand?"

With disgust and shame, Ben saw the logic behind Doyle's actions. He felt sick. "I understand."

"I had to save them," Doyle muttered. "No one else would have. I'm the only one who could do it. I had to save them from communion."

"By killing them," Ben said. A metallic taste formed at the back of his mouth.

Doyle nodded, his eyes wide and scared. "I made it quick for them. I didn't let them suffer. Now they're at peace."

"You can't kill kids, Doyle," said Ben. "You don't kill kids. Do you realise what you've done?"

"Of course." Doyle's voice was so reedy and pathetic that Ben wanted to take out the man's tongue. "All that matters now is how we die. I had to kill Fenrir too. Had to shoot him. It was a mercy. A quick death for a loyal friend. But he didn't understand when he looked up at me as I put the barrel to his head. I saw it in his eyes. But I had to do it. Then I buried him in the garden with his favourite chew toy, and made a marker for his grave. Now he's at peace, just like the children."

Ben put his hands to his face.

"I had to save as many as I could. The vulnerable, the little ones. But I can't take any more lives. I can't do it."

"This is madness," Ben said. "Put the gun down. Please, Doyle."

The other man shook his head, all fight leaving him. "I knew you'd come to see me before the end, Ben. I'm tired. I have nothing left."

Ben would have tried to dissuade Doyle, but he was tired, too, and he had to let Doyle have control of his own fate. Better than being gunned down by the police or lynched by the villagers. And as much as he hated Doyle for killing the children, he fully understood why Doyle had done it. Such clarity was abhorrent at that moment.

Ben nodded at him. "Do what you have to do, Doyle."

"Thank you, Ben. I didn't want to be alone at the end. I appreciate it." A slow, exhausted sigh escaped his mouth and he gripped the rifle tightly. "Life is a hideous thing."

Ben stepped back.

Doyle put the barrel into his mouth, breathing past the black metal in heaving sobs. He set his eyes upon the ceiling, to look away from the red slaughter upon the classroom floor.

~

After the deafening crack of the rifle, Ben stood there for a long while. Doyle had collapsed in a broken heap, legs twitching and splayed, and the shattered back of his skull and what had been inside stuck to the wall in a scattered wet pattern of bone fragments, pulped red and glistening grey. Ben, despite himself, pitied Doyle. He sat on the floor among the left behind toys and picture books and covered his face with numb hands. The room was silent in the aftermath of the gunshot, but he thought he heard children giggling and whispering out in the corridor beyond the classroom. He ignored them, realising it was only his exhausted, tortured mind playing games with him.

The clock on the wall ticked away its last seconds and then stopped.

Ben only raised his head when footsteps scraped and dragged behind him, and before he turned, he was smothered by hands and limbs and stinking rags over his screaming mouth.

Nineteen

You see the empty cities, towns and villages. Dust, ash, bone, rust and atrophy. A silent, dead world. You see the entity emerge through the membrane of worlds, all shapeless and immense. It forms into a black star and spreads madness and death. A gathering of pulsing black light. Dark matter. A planet-killer. Something beyond your understanding. A thing newly-born into this world. It brings communion.

You see the destroyer of worlds. The black sun. Absorbing all life and the knowledge of an entire species. All that we achieved and created, all our accomplishments and progress. All of it wiped away like drawings in the sand. No one left to remember us. The monuments we built will stand for centuries, maybe millennia, until the wind scours them from the earth, and the human race will be a memory of a dream dreamed by the stars. An evolutionary line ended by annihilation.

You see the Earth as a barren world, gone the way of other planets and the species that once lived upon them. One day, with nothing left to bear witness, our star will die and our world will be consumed by the final rage of the dwindling sun. Inevitable. None of this will matter.

All of it will be dust.

~

In what may be a dream or vision, his father crouches over him and concern makes the old man appear wizened and cadaverous. He places one hand on Ben's shoulder. A small smile, barely a movement of his mouth. Almost nothing. And there is sadness in his eyes.

"I couldn't leave you behind, son."

~

Ben came back to the world gasping for air. An incessant metallic ringing filled his ears, and above that were the sounds of screaming and crying around him. Bonfires were burning in the fields. His mouth worked until the cramp in his chest alleviated and his lungs bloomed with oxygen. He sucked on air until his jaw ached. The snow had stopped in the late afternoon, and the light was beginning to fade. People from the village littered the fields. Many of them were curled foetal on the ground, trembling and pale, frothing past their mouths. Others were crawling along the snow-dusted ground, muttering and crying. Some of them stood unmoving and staring at the sky beyond Ben.

On his knees, he turned around, and his heart almost stopped. The air was pinched from his lungs and he staggered until he stopped next to a sobbing woman.

Halfway between the white heavens and the

curve of the horizon, the black star was bleeding into the sky, fully emerged. It filled most of the sky like a rogue moon passing too close to the Earth. It was rimmed by branching tendrils spread outwards to splinter and darken the sky.

Shadows were running like paint. Ben covered his ears against the shriek of screaming metal and the grind of tectonic plates. The songs of the abyss.

A flock of starlings fell from the sky.

Ben felt something at the very core of him cower and shrink away. The acknowledgement of something so far beyond his species that to simply witness it brought nihilism and despair.

Our extinction happens between the rise and fall of the black star.

Ben wiped at his mouth until his lips were raw.

Around him were tortured cries from yawning mouths. Wailing and screaming. People confused, disorientated and terrified. The fear of herd animals led to slaughter. He could hear children crying, and hysterical laughter from somewhere nearby. The bawling of infants for their mothers. Meat all around him. The ringing was growing louder; men and women covered their ears with their hands and cried. A man sprawling on the ground, close to Ben, was having a seizure, foaming and trembling. Other people were wailing towards the sky and the black star, their arms held aloft.

Ben struggled to his feet. He glimpsed men and women scratching at their skin until thin strips of it peeled away. An old woman was crying into hands that were almost skeletal.

The metallic ringing grew louder, filled his head, and turned his legs to straw and sticks. He covered his ears with his forearms, but the ringing had burrowed into his mind and made a warm, damp nest there. He vomited hot steaming bile onto the frozen field then fell to his knees and looked at the black star, tears in his eyes, tremors in his limbs. He wept like a child, terrified and awestruck. Light flashed, strobe-like, and the sky roared. Lovely lightning. The echo of cosmic voices. He had to turn away. Needles in his brain, nails in his spine, and thorns in his skull.

A small herd of deer scattered across the fields, away from the burning black star. The nearby woods echoed with frightened animal cries and barks.

Ben fled from the fields and did not look at the sky.

Twenty

Into the village. Some people were in their gardens staring above them and covering their ears against the constant ringing. They ignored Ben as he staggered through the streets. A family threw bags and suitcases into a car and drove away. Many of the houses were abandoned, their owners gone off to the fields. Doors hung open like waiting mouths.

The sky was darkening, but not because of the approaching night. Ben's ears hurt and his head pounded. He didn't stop moving; if he stopped, he would never get up again. He ran past a crying man sitting on the pavement. There was a gunshot from one of the houses. Dogs barked and howled.

Smoke poured from the church. Flames glimpsed behind the stained glass windows.

Ben passed the school where children had died.

Some people were catatonic in the street, heads bowed and unmoving.

The sound of mountains falling came from beyond the village. The detonations of imploding suns. The deep crackle of thunder. The sky was moving. Nuclear wind. The black star was rising. Ben pawed at his ears and his skull. He let tears run down his face.

He screamed until his vocal chords were scraped raw.

~

Ben arrived at the house. He looked at it for a moment, trying to picture his parents in the front garden, sat in their deckchairs, sipping lemonade and reading in the sun while listening to the radio.

He wiped tears from his eyes.

One last time up the garden path and through the doorway. He stood in his bedroom, which he would never see again. He touched the wall and closed his eyes, running his fingers over the fractures and cracks in the plaster. He watched a spider scurry into a slit where the walls met and he wished it well. He collected his personal belongings and whatever food was left in the cupboards then filled a bottle with water from the tap.

He went through Mum's old photo albums until he found an image of his parents together. He took a few trinkets and some memories – things to help him remember.

Above the house, the sky crackled. The light was fading.

He packed his medication and a packet of Ibuprofen, dumped it all in a rucksack that might have once been the bag he took to school when he was a boy. Then he tried the television, but it was dead, and when he flicked the light switches the house remained dark.

Ben stood in the silent rooms of the house and said goodbye. He wanted to remember the house – his home – as a place of warmth and comfort, not as it was now, empty and dead, a shell made of fading walls and pale ceilings.

He locked the house after he left. Placed one hand on the front door before he walked down the garden path under the alien sky. He climbed in the car and placed the rucksack on the front passenger's seat, then glimpsed himself in the rear-view mirror and almost gasped at his thin, shivering face and bloodshot eyes. He slotted the key in the ignition. The engine struggled to life. He switched on the radio, but there was only static upon the airwaves no matter which frequency he tried.

The sky sounded like it was falling.

Ben looked at the house for the last time and then drove away. He crept through the village, along its roads and through its waning streets. Everything empty and silent. A few people must have fled, but most of the population was out in the fields, waiting for communion.

He hoped his father died quickly, if he wasn't already dead. He would never know, and it was for the best.

Ben left it all behind.

Epilogue

When Ben slept he dreamed of terrible things, so he tried to stay awake for as long as he could.

He headed northwards through the mist of grey lands below charcoal skies. Ash fell from a thousand fires.

The car's engine stuttered. The radio snapped terrified voices and the whispers of old friends. There were dead animals by the roadsides, but hardly any scavengers to prosper from the carrion. He hadn't seen another person in two days.

The black star filled the sky, now, and the world was darkened in its shadow. Nuclear winter. Life was being absorbed. Communion given to billions. The sun had vanished days ago. A fire burned in a distant field, flames taller than the dying trees.

Almost ready to join his brothers and sisters in extinction, Ben stopped the car when he was certain he'd found the right place. He left the car by the roadside, where it would rust and dwindle into the years, opened the gate to the field and walked into the long grass that reached his knees. The mist was foul-smelling. Bad air. He wondered if the Earth's atmosphere was changing. The grass was dying, yellowed and damp and cloying with the stink of rot.

He was worried he was at the wrong place until Trench Hill appeared ahead of him out of the mist. He sagged with relief and allowed a smile upon his mouth.

There were snapping-wood sounds off in the mist, and what might have been voices. But he knew better than that. He knew to ignore them.

He walked to the top of the hill.

The tree was still standing, but it was skeletal and blackened, weeping with sickness. Bare branches wilted and twisted. It didn't matter.

There were small bones in the grass around his feet.

Ben sat with his back against the tree, looking out over the mist-covered fields. He guessed, by his skewed sense of direction, the locations of the dark stains of towns and villages and what they had become. The world was silent. The black star had gorged itself; now it was picking through the remains.

Ben opened the rucksack and took out his last belongings. A half-empty bottle of vodka, a packet of cigarettes, boxes of antidepressants and assorted painkillers he'd looted from a chemist's. And, finally, his photos.

He set everything out on the grass before him. He looked at the photo of his parents. A photo of him and Emily on the hill, with the tree behind them, where he had proposed to her a thousand years ago. The tree had been heavy with leaves that day and the sun had been high above them.

He kissed her frozen image then placed the photo on the grass. Distant sounds were approaching, and he looked out to the grey land. His god was coming to find him, but he wasn't afraid anymore and he wondered what communion felt like, if that was to be his fate.

His heart was slow and stable as he chased each pill with a tip of the bottle. He stopped counting after fifteen. Better to have too much than not enough.

His eyelids were heavy as he reclined against the tree, lit his final cigarette in steady hands, and smiled at the last memory of his wife.

This time he would sleep, but he wouldn't dream.

Rich Hawkins hails from the depths of Somerset, England, where a childhood of science fiction and horror films set him on the path to writing his own stories. He credits his love of horror and all things weird to his first viewing of John Carpenter's THE THING back in the early Nineties. His debut novel THE LAST PLAGUE was nominated for a British Fantasy Award for Best Horror Novel in 2015.

CPSIA information can be obtained
at www.ICGtesting.com
Printed in the USA
LVHW091635110220
646416LV00072B/339